OUT
TO FIND
FREEDOM

LILA ROSE
USA TODAY BESTSELLING AUTHOR

AUTHOR'S NOTE

STOP. Before you read on, I highly suggest for you to listen to a song called "Beautiful Crazy" by Luke Combs. You'll know why when you get to the part. It's also the only song I listened to when writing this story.

Out to Find Freedom starts out intense and dark, then moves into a very slow burn romance. It's also set six months after No Way Out (Stoke and Malinda's story from the Hawks MC: Ballarat Charter) but it can be read as a standalone.

CHAPTER ONE

EMERSON

*W*hen my sixty-year-old father died six months ago, it was the day I stopped living. It honestly felt like my world ended in that ambulance when he took his last breath. He'd been my father, my friend, and my confidant all rolled into one.

Life wasn't fair.

My heart still ached. Like, with every breath I took, my chest compressed painfully, as if wrapped tightly by a boa constrictor.

I didn't remember my mother. She passed away when I was two from a snake bite. Living out on a property meant we'd been too far away to get help. By the time the ambulance arrived, she was gone. At least, that was what my dad told me, and he was a man I believed with my whole heart.

When dad passed, I had no one except Gloria, my mum's younger sister who was twenty-five—eight years older than I was—and her sleazy boyfriend, Lenny, who was around the same age as Gloria. I didn't actually know because I didn't really care. Dad and I had nothing to do with Gloria. I knew nothing about the woman beyond what Dad had told me. That she was a young fool, and always in trouble with the law after her and Mum's parents died a year apart of one another.

I couldn't even bring myself to call her my aunt. To me, she wasn't family. I only had one person who was, and he was gone.

Thankfully, my estranged family kept to themselves and let me mourn. My routine was set in stone since the day I moved in with them. Go to school, back to the house, make myself dinner, eat it in my room, study, and go to sleep.

When I'd first walked through their door, they'd told me I could do what I wanted, but I had to be home by nine, in bed by ten, and make sure I cleaned up after myself. Gloria then went on with a bored expression and said she wasn't my slave, so I would be making my own meals. Which I was fine with. I'd been independent for many years since Dad would be busy taking care of the land on our fifty acres.

One year and I could be out of the place.

One year and I would be old enough to live on my own. I was going to use the money Dad's life insurance paid out, also what he had in his bank account, and then there was the amount I had saved from helping him out around the property, to get away from them.

Then in seven years, I would have access to my inheritance.

Dad wasn't stupid. He'd known how to invest his money, and it had paid off. By the time I turned twenty-five, I would be a millionaire.

Only I would have given it all up, *all* the money, if I could have kept my father with me.

"Hey, how about we head to the lake and chat?"

I wanted to groan, but I withheld it and turned to Donny. Why I agreed to a date in the first place, I didn't know. I was seriously thinking of getting my sanity checked. Though, I did have a little red-haired devil sitting on my shoulder, which often encouraged me to do some daft shit. Harriet White, a close friend from my new school, had talked me into giving Donny a chance. In fact, she'd begged me to because he was best mates with Walt, the guy she was interested in.

However, with Donny bringing up the lake, the known make-out place, I knew he only wanted one thing, and I wasn't about to give it to him.

"No thanks. I'm not feeling the best." I had to sit through an hour of him talking about football. I was about ready to fall asleep. "I only live up the road. Do you think you could take me home?"

He frowned. "I thought you were staying at Harriet's?"

Damn, I was supposed to. I even dropped my bag off at her place, but right then I didn't want to face her and all her questions.

"Yes, but if I am coming down with something, I don't want to stay there. I'll text her." I took out my phone and waved it in my hand.

"Fine." He sighed.

Me: Sorry, can't stay. Not feeling well. Must have ate something bad.

Harriet: WHAT? No way, you have to tell me how it went.

Me: Tomorrow at school. Promise.

Harriet: I'm eye rolling so hard right now.

I didn't bother replying since Donny was already driving up my street. "Just in the next block, number eight."

He hummed under his breath. When he pulled up, he turned off his car. "I'll walk you in."

That was sweet but unnecessary. "You don't have to—"

"Emerson, just let me."

"Okay," I whispered, and suddenly felt bad for not being

attracted to him. He'd been nice to pick me up at Harriet's, opened doors for me, made sure I was happy with the place we ate at. But I didn't feel a connection.

Maybe I was broken.

I didn't want to put all the blame on Donny because he talked and talked about a sport he was obviously into. I was at fault as well. I'd let myself be pressured into a date with him when I wasn't in the right frame of mind.

When he walked around the car, I quickly opened my door and got out before he reached it. "I'm sorry about tonight."

"Yeah?"

"Yes. I…" I shrugged. "I know it's been a while since my father died, but it still hurts, and I can't see past the pain just yet. Maybe when I can, we could revisit this?"

Finally, he was back to smiling. "I'd like that."

In the meantime, I would hope someone else caught his attention. At least we weren't leaving the night on a sour feeling. We walked slowly to the front door, Donny's hand on my lower back. He was such an old-school gentleman, and I was kicking myself for not liking football. Maybe then we'd have a better connection.

However, I wasn't in the mood to force anything between us. Thankfully he wasn't forcing the subject.

Turning at the door on the front porch, I smiled. "Thank you for dinner."

"You're welcome. I hope you feel better soon."

I gave him a thin-lipped grin and nodded. "So do I."

"Do you mind if I kiss your cheek?"

See, he was such a sweetheart.

"I don't mind." His smile was bright. Gently, his hands landed on my shoulders. He leaned in and softly laid his lips against my cheek.

When my body didn't react in any type of way, I wanted to punch myself.

He shifted back, still smiling. I reached out for the door handle and twisted, checking it wasn't locked. "Well, thanks again."

"Thanks for coming."

I pushed the door open, ready to step through backwards to stop feeling awkward. Only a scream ripped from my mouth when my neck was gripped hard. My body got yanked backwards. I saw Donny's eyes widen, and he yelled, "Hey!" and came my way.

Only once he was through the door, it got slammed closed.

Silence.

For all but a beat, until I cried out when I was forcefully pushed to the floor, landing on my knees.

"What the fuck? What the fuck?" Gloria, my aunt, ranted in front of me.

It was then that I took in the room. In all of a second, I saw a younger teen lying on the couch half-naked. She seemed out of it. A man stood before her doing up his pants. There was a camera, extra lights, and two other men in the room. One was Lenny, my aunt's boyfriend.

"Get to your knees" was growled out. I looked back to Donny and the man behind him.

No. No, no, no. A gun was pointed at Donny's head. He sank to his knees. His eyes, brimming with tears, were on me.

"Please, please, just let him go," I begged.

My hair was gripped, my head jerked back. Gloria got in my face. "You weren't supposed to be here." She shook my head roughly using my hair.

"Please, let him go," I pleaded. Bringing my arms up, I used my shaking hands to hold her tee. "Please. He won't say anything."

"I won't," Donny whispered.

"Fuck!" Gloria yelled. She dropped her hold on me and spun to face the others. "We should have gone to the warehouse."

"Babe, you know we couldn't. It's hot. Got people watching it."

"We need to find somewhere else," the man behind Donny said. "But...." He glanced down at Donny.

Gloria ran her hands through her hair. Then she nodded.

"No!" I screamed, but it was too late.

I didn't even hear the gun. All I saw was Donny's body fall to the floor. He didn't breathe. Didn't blink. Didn't move. His lifeless eyes stared my way.

I gagged. Dropping to my hands on the carpet, I heaved. I couldn't drag my eyes away from him. Donny. I'd killed him. It was my fault.

Blood soaked the carpet. *His* blood dripped from the hole in his head.

Another heave erupted as tears ran down my cheeks. My body shook, and a noise hit my ears. Whimpering and keening. I realised it was coming from me.

"What about her?" someone asked. I didn't care who. I didn't look. All I could see was Donny. Dead before me.

My fault.

All my fault.

Because he wanted to go on a date with me, and now he was dead for it.

"Shut up" was roared.

I clamped my lips closed, but I couldn't stop the whimpers, the tears. My throat thickened, and I heaved again.

"We can't kill her."

"Why the fuck not?" he demanded. Gloria stomped over to

him and dragged him into a corner for a huddled whispered conversation.

Slowly, I crawled to Donny. "I'm sorry, I'm sorry, I'm so, so sorry," I uttered. I started to reach out to him but pulled my hand back.

The blood. It was everywhere. My body shook. My chest ached in such a painful way that it caught my breath.

A new whimper caught my attention. I glanced behind me to the girl on the couch. She moved but then stilled once more.

"We got to get her out of here before she wakes."

The man with Gloria, who seemed in charge, grunted. "You and Lenny take her. Dump her in an alley somewhere."

"W-what did you do to her?" It was obvious, and yet I didn't really want to know or hear their answer. But I couldn't help asking.

"She knows too much," the guy with Lenny said.

"Gloria has a plan," Lenny said.

"Maybe she'd let her be in the next movie."

Lenny smirked. "That I'd pay to see."

I cringed at his dark look and scooted back on the floor. While they dressed the girl, my eyes drifted to the front door. I could run, scream, fight.

Jean-clad legs entered my view. It was the man who'd been talking with Gloria. "Don't even fucking think about it. If it was up to me, you'd be dead."

Dead.

Like Donny.

I heaved, then vomited onto the carpet. A boot landed in my side, and I grunted and gasped. People yelled, argued, but I couldn't hear any of it.

My ears rang as thought after thought screamed into my mind.

Gloria, my aunt, was a part of something so vile it churned my stomach again, and I let another load of spew loose.

A girl was drugged. Raped. Filmed.

Here. In the house. She was violated in a way no woman or man should be.

I had to do something.

For her.

For Donny.

The man stepped away from me to roll Donny's body over. Gloria stood with Lenny and the rapist arguing. They were distracted.

I took the chance.

For the girl and Donny.

Knowing I could end up like either one of them.

Wiping my mouth with the back of my hand, I flashed up and ran for the door. The man tried to grab for me, yelled. I made it, touched the door handle... and then saw nothing but stars.

Somehow I ended up flat on my back on the floor. I blinked slowly, my vision dimming as I looked up at Gloria with a baseball bat in her hand.

"You really shouldn't have done that. Take her to the basement," she ordered, just before everything faded.

CHAPTER TWO

EMERSON

For over a month, I'd been in the basement. Tears always remained close to the edge, and I lost count of the times I would break. It was only the previous day when Gloria unchained me so I could move around the room more instead of being only near the bed and to reach the toilet. I learned my lesson to stop shouting and screaming. I needed to move more, and the way I got the privilege was to keep quiet. So I did.

The night *it* happened, when I woke in the basement on the floor, Gloria had been crouched over me. She told me I had to be good, or I would end up dead. If that didn't give me enough incentive, she then informed me that she used my fingerprint to get into my phone. Gloria read my messages, looked at everything, and in the end, my aunt threatened Harriet's and her family's lives if I didn't do as I was told. She mentioned how she messaged Harriet pretending to be me and told her things to make sure she got the picture I wouldn't be back at that school. Gloria didn't tell me what Harriet replied with, so I didn't know if she believed Gloria's lies… or "my" lies.

Harriet knew Donny more than I did. She'd suspect something was wrong when he didn't show for school too. Unless they had that covered. I didn't have a clue.

Honestly, I couldn't understand how or why no police showed. I didn't know for certain what Gloria had said to the school or authorities about me, or if they came looking for clues to Donny's disappearance.

God. Donny.

They killed Donny.

Right there in front of me.

They killed him… all because of me.

Because I came home.

Guilt ate at my insides each and every day.

Nothing like this seemed like it could happen in reality, but it had. I was a part of it. Gloria and Lenny were bad, toxic people. How and why they did what they did was a shock to my core. I could never understand the reason for sinking to an act only the Devil himself would love. How many girls had suffered? How many were taken, drugged, defiled, and dumped? Remembered nothing beyond knowing they'd been touched?

Just the thought of my so-called family had bile rising in my throat. The knowledge twisted and tore at my stomach.

I wanted them gone.

Dead.

I wished I could make it happen. They deserved to die for what they'd done.

Standing from the camp bed they'd provided, I walked over to one of the many boxes in the corner in the hope it would give me some type of weapon; over the time, I had only managed to go through half of them because there were that many. Only I knew they wouldn't be so stupid to leave something down here like that. When I opened the box, I saw nothing but clothes, old magazines, and records. Another one showed me piles of wool, but no knitting needles. The ones I'd already opened were similar to the others, nothing that could help me.

Though, when I moved to a smaller one, I found some notepads, two pencils, a pen, and some romantic paperbacks.

I huffed out a breath and wiped at my eyes again. Maybe I could read them to death or stab them with a pencil before they could kill me.

Useless.

That was how I felt.

Utterly useless.

Why were they keeping me around? Why hadn't they killed me like Donny?

Why did they even have to kill Donny?

I should have fought more. Saved him somehow.

A sob caught in my throat. I moved to the tiny basin in the toilet room under the stairs and washed my face, trying to get my emotions under control. I knew it wouldn't last. I had nothing but time to think about what had happened. About seeing Donny's lifeless eyes stare at me.

I gripped the sink. Another sob had my body jerking.

This wasn't fair.

None of it.

I stormed from the room and flicked my hand out at a box. The box crashed to the floor. I kicked another and it flew forwards. I picked up another and threw it across the room. I screamed, yelled, and cried. My pain took over as I gripped my hair and tugged.

Why Donny?

Why that girl?

Why did Dad die?

Why was I left here?

Why wasn't anyone coming to help?

Why, why, why?

Another scream rattled out. I dropped to my knees and pounded my fists against the concrete floor.

I didn't care if they came down. I wanted them to. I wanted to punch, kick, stab, and hurt them in every way. They needed to feel the pain I was in, the pain they inflicted on others.

Only there weren't any footsteps… so when I heard a tapping sound, I stopped still, and through the tears, I looked up and over to the small rectangle window, the size of a book, above my bed.

There, on her knees, was Mrs Minna. The eighty-something next-door neighbour.

I shook my head. "No," I whispered. If they saw her, they wouldn't let her go. Snapping up to my feet, I rushed over to the window. Standing on the bed, I unlocked it and pushed it the few inches open it would allow. "Go. Please, go," I begged. Fear clutched at my chest. If Gloria or Lenny heard, the risk of it was unthinkable. Harm would come to me, Mrs Minna, or Harriet. I couldn't let any of it happen.

"I knew you didn't run off. I'm going to call the police. Wait there—"

"Mrs Minna, please don't, they'll—no!" I screamed. Lenny came up behind Mrs Minna. His hands wrapped around her head, and he snapped it quickly to the side.

I saw the shock in her eyes before nothing.

Dead.

Blank. Like Donny's had been.

Because of me.

"You fucking cunt," I screeched. I tried to reach for Lenny through the window. Of course it was fucking useless. Just like I was.

My body rocked to the side from a force to my waist.

Something cracked on the inside. I could feel it, hear it, all before I hit the ground hard. I rolled to the side, wincing, whimpering, and crying to see Gloria standing over me.

"You fucking bitch. We leave to get some shit and you're calling out to the neighbour. Her death, like your friend's, is on you."

I sat up and cried out, grabbing my side just below my breast. Gloria snorted. "Probably cracked a rib or two. Your fucking fault. All of it. Damn, everything is your fault."

Through a panting breath, I wheezed, "Y-you killed her. Police will know."

Shaking her head, she rolled her eyes. Kicking out at my foot, she told me, "Don't be stupid. Lenny's already taking her body to her house. I told him to snap her neck. Those stairs in her house aren't good for an eighty-year-old. Really dangerous, actually. She's likely to fall down them and break her neck.... Huh, guess it just happened." She laughed.

Gloria was a lunatic. She wasn't only crazy but vicious.

How did she become the way she was?

Dad had told me Mum's parents had been nice people. The only option I could guess was drugs had screwed Gloria up.

But still, with not knowing how drugs worked, did they really cause a person to become a disgusting monster like Gloria?

"Why?"

"No one fucks with my life. Least of all Marilee's little precious Emerson. You need to understand I don't give a fuck you're my sister's daughter. I didn't care about her. I don't care about you. What I care about is Lenny, money, and making sure people do as I say. I get paid for what I do, but my boss even knows to do what *I* say. Especially when I bring money into the business game." She smiled. "Thanks to you and your bank account."

My chest clenched. "T-that's my dad's."

That money was what I would have lived on until I turned twenty-five. It was his life insurance and his money from his account. It was meant to help me.

She'd stolen it.

Stolen another part of my dad.

She'd already taken his watch, something I accused her of, but she blamed me for misplacing it.

She may as well take me.

End me and my misery.

"Kill me," I whispered.

Her head dropped back and she laughed up at the ceiling. Her arm wound around her waist as she kept laughing. Her humour waning, she shook her head and looked down at me with hostility. "Another thing you'll learn. You die when *I* say." She brought the bat up and swung it. I closed my eyes cringing, waiting. When nothing happened, I peeked out to see her smiling once more down at me. She scoffed. "Pathetic. She should have killed you in her womb." She turned and walked away.

I didn't move. Instead, I listened until I heard the basement door bang closed. I knew I wouldn't be getting any food that night, and honestly, I didn't think I could eat.

They killed again because of me.

Another life lost, and it was my fault.

When would this nightmare end?

If I had a knife, had something sharp, I would end it all myself.

Then again, I probably would be too weak to do it.

Maybe she was right. I was pathetic.

Slowly, I got to my knees as my anguished cries for Mrs Minna turned into pain stabbing through my side. I crawled to the bed and slid into it, breathing harshly.

Mrs Minna may have been eighty, nearing the end of her time on earth, but she didn't deserve to have it end so quickly. She had children, grandkids. Ones she'd spoken of the first time I met her. She'd heard why I'd moved in with Gloria and had felt sorry for me. She even asked me in for a cup of tea and cookies. I didn't accept, but I was grateful for the offer. Grateful she'd cared enough to ask. Gloria hadn't cared when they'd brought me here. She never asked if I was okay, yet a stranger had. Mrs Minna was a good soul, and now she was lost to the world, to her family.

I should have gone in. I should have gotten to know her.

Now it was too late.

Because of me.

A cough jerked my body and I cried out, curling into myself, holding my side.

I wasn't lying when I told her to kill me. I wished she would.

Then the pain would stop.

The hurt would end along with my life.

Maybe then I would see my dad, even my mum, again.

CHAPTER THREE

EMERSON

*N*oise woke me from my sleep. Blinking slowly, I rolled on the tiny bed, the one I'd slept on for the last couple of years, and peered out the small window to the real world. What the window showed was the neighbour's house. What used to be Mrs Minna's house before…. Hers was a little shorter in length than Gloria's, so through the wired fence, I had a view of the back corner of the house, the deck, and some of the backyard.

Sleepiness evaporated when I saw people walking up and down the side of the house and in the backyard. I quickly ducked, my breath catching in my throat.

With shaky hands, I placed them on the windowsill and cautiously peeked out. Men, women, and even children of all ages walked by, carrying things such as deck furniture, computers, TVs.

Someone was moving in.

No one had lived next door since Mrs Minna was murdered. Though, Gloria had been right; the authorities didn't class it as murder. It had been an accident—an old lady falling down her stairs. Where Lenny had laid her body after he'd broken her neck.

Clenching my jaw, I shook the threatening dark thoughts away. Finally I had something to watch, to listen to. Their voices were a little muffled, until I slowly and carefully reached up and unlatched the window. I pushed it out as far as it went, which wasn't far since it had been made to stay closed enough so nothing, nor no one, could get in or out.

Their voices cleared, especially when I stood on the camp bed and tilted my ear to the window.

When others went back out the front or through the back door, a man stood there with a woman and a teen boy. He said, "It's a nice joint."

"It's a little big. Four bedrooms for one man," the woman commented.

"Maybe he's got a woman we don't know about," the teen boy added with a cheeky grin.

The first man snorted. "Good. Means he'll stop checkin' my woman out."

"Declan." She sighed. "Ryan and I are just friends. You know this already."

"Ryan? Since fuckin' when did you start callin' him Ryan?" the man demanded. He sounded very angry; I wouldn't want to cross him.

Only the woman didn't seem fazed by his tone. She put her box down on the back deck and waved her hand around aimlessly. "Since after the trouble I had."

"Mum," the boy groaned. "You say 'trouble' like it was something small. You were poisoned and kidnapped."

I sucked down a shocked breath. Poisoned and taken?

"It was nearly six months ago," the woman pointed out. She made it sound as if it was years, not months.

The man dropped his box, glared at the woman, and stormed back around the front of the house. Out of my sight.

"Maybe we shouldn't talk about it in front of Declan," the woman suggested.

"*Maybe* you shouldn't be blasé about it, Mum," the boy snapped.

The woman stepped over to him, took the box out of his arms, and placed it down. She cupped his cheeks. My heart gave a lurch at her gentleness.

"I know. I'm sorry. Promise I won't make light of it again."

He nodded, she smiled, and then they hugged, but the teen pushed her away when more people came down the side.

Moving back, I leaned against the wall. My chest rose and fell rapidly.

I wanted that.

A family who cared.

But I no longer had anyone who would.

I understood why God wanted to take Dad away. He was wonderful, caring, and just an amazing person. God probably needed him for some saintly duty.

But it left me alone.

Alone to deal with Gloria and Lenny. Both of them didn't have a caring, nice bone in their body.

Never would have I known just how things would change in my life after losing Dad.

I hadn't known the hell I would be forced into.

Hadn't realised people could be so cruel, disgusting, and sadistic.

But there were people like that.

And I was under the same roof with two of them.

They hated me. I had something over them, something that could destroy them like they deserved. I didn't understand why they didn't kill me already, until about six months ago when Lenny was being loud and talking shit on the phone.

"Yeah, brother, we still got her. You want a piece of her?" He paused. My throat closed over to keep the bile from rising. "Ha, you being funny. Nah, she'd be pure. You'd have to pay a mil' or I might just have a go myself." I clutched my stomach. "We're keepin' her until she gets her inheritance. We want the big, fat pile of money; then she's dead. So you got some time to make up your mind. Six years."

It was a few weeks after that call when I found out what Lenny meant by "having a go himself." I'd been sitting on the bed in the dark, just glancing up at the sky, waiting for a falling star to wish upon. It sounded ridiculous, but my luck had ended the day Dad died, and I thought just once, some miracle could happen and I would awaken from this nightmare.

A few seconds after, I learned luck was a crock of shit.

I'd heard the front door burst open. I'd jolted and gripped my knees to my chest tighter. Closing my eyes, I'd prayed the staggering footsteps would continue to the bedrooms.

But they stopped.

Just outside the basement door.

The door banged open, and Lenny stumbled down the stairs. "'Dere she is," he'd slurred.

My body chilled, noticing his hungry eyes running over me. My heart spiked.

I hated it.

He'd always creeped me out.

Slowly, I'd stood from the bed in preparation to bolt and stammered, "I-I'm going to sleep."

What was worse, I knew my aunt hadn't been home. From the silence of the house earlier, I'd thought it was one of those rare occasions she'd gone out with Lenny.

He'd smirked and stepped closer. "Sleep sounds good."

I'd brought my hands up as he stepped towards me. "Lenny, don't—" I'd screamed as he lurched forward, his hand gripping my long dark hair and pulling me towards him. His lips had landed on mine, hard. I'd pushed, hit, and tried to knee. For a drunk man, he'd still been able to fight off everything I did.

When he'd pushed me, I'd fallen back to the cot and gone to scramble off and run, but he was on me. I'd screamed in his face, and he'd laughed. I'd gotten an arm free and elbowed him in the jaw. Immediately, he'd grabbed it and forced it down, then rolled me. My knees hit the floor hard.

"Don't! Please don't do this," I'd cried. Tears had streamed down my face.

Fear like I'd never felt twisted my insides.

"Shh." He'd petted my hair with one hand while the other pushed down my shorts. "You want this." He'd leaned over me. Bile choked me. His rancid breath had fanned my face with his next words. "You tell her, I'll kill you."

But I didn't have to tell Gloria.

She'd come down the stairs, took it all in within seconds, and bounded over. She pulled Lenny back, slapped him so hard he fell back to his butt. He'd started pleading with her, telling her it was my fault, that I called him down and came on to him.

In my shock, I'd crawled away from them both yelling at each other. My ears ringing, my body shaking, I'd sobbed and curled into a corner.

It was stupid to think for a second that Gloria was my aunt, that she would take care of me, would kick him out.

My eyes had sprung wide as I'd felt a fist in my hair again. Gloria dragged me by my locks to the stairs and up them while I'd struggled with her hold. Her words that I caught through my cries hadn't made sense. "This is your fault.... You shouldn't have ruined my life.... You took his attention away from me."

She'd opened the bathroom door, dragged me in. Even though I fought to break away by kicking, twisting, and punching, she'd been stronger.

With her hand in my hair, she'd shoved me to the side. Gloria then bent down. "Shut up," she'd roared in my face.

My lips clamped tight. Still, I'd tried. "Gloria, w-what are you doing?" I'd sat on the floor, arms wrapped around my legs, shaking, breaking. She had the cupboard open, searching for something. I'd gone to put my arms down, try and move from the room as she'd mumbled to herself over and over. Only as soon as I'd moved, her glassy eyes shot down to me. Her pupils had been bigger than I'd ever seen them. Something had been wrong with her.

"Don't move," she'd snapped harshly.

"Glory, honey, what're you doing?" Lenny had asked in the doorway.

She'd turned to him, took two steps his way, and slammed the door in his face. Once she locked it, she'd faced me. My throat had thickened at what I saw in her hand. I'd moved back quickly, until I hit the wall.

"No, no, no," I'd chanted as she came at me. "No!" I'd screamed when her blade sliced my arm.

"Keep fucking still or I'll slice your throat," she'd screeched.

Hard sobs jolted my body, but I'd kept my lips closed. I'd screwed my eyes shut and whimpered through her cutting my arms over and over.

"Once I'm through with you, he won't look at you again. Thinks he likes your body. He won't after this." She'd laughed.

She didn't stop at my arms.

My aunt carved at my chest, my legs, and stomach, then left

me on the floor crying, bleeding, and dying on the inside once more.

The only grace of that night was when Gloria left the bathroom, stating for me to clean up my mess and get back down to the basement. If I didn't, she was going to hunt down Harriet and kill her. From everything I'd seen and experienced, I knew her threats were true.

After I wrapped myself up as much as I could, I'd stumbled out of the room, down the dirty, messy hall where I'd spotted my old handbag on the floor. I couldn't believe they stupidly just thrown it to the ground and it was still there after all of this time. My pulse had ticked over quickly. She must have dumped it there after she got my fingerprint to message Harriet and my bank card PIN number. Immediately I'd wondered if my phone and charger might still be in there.

Gloria had been in the living room yelling at Lenny. He had been screaming back just as much. Soon that meant they'd be screwing each other, so I'd had to be quick. Bending, my skin pulling, I bit down on my bottom lip to stop myself crying out. I'd looked inside it and found my phone and charger. I left the bag where it had been in case she noticed it gone. It was doubtful though, considering the unkempt state the house was in.

I didn't know what I was going to do with my phone. Calling for help had not been an option; I couldn't risk Harriet's life for mine. Gloria and Lenny had already used the threat of killing her and her family if anyone was to find out what they'd been up to or if a cop came to the door. Their people were only one text or phone call away, and they would get it done without ever being caught. So my charged phone sat hidden for the day I knew both of them would be out and I could think of a plan to save Harriet, her family, and myself.

If only I could remember her number, but they'd wiped my

phone clear of everything. At least they hadn't been smart enough to end the direct debit payments for the bill from my account. Or they just didn't care enough to look since they had a good supply of money to use.

They'd even deleted my old photos of my father.

A new voice caught my attention, dragging me away from my thoughts, and for that, I was grateful.

"Yo, Warden, where you gonna put this garden shit?"

I peeked out the window and that was when I saw him.

He walked—no, strode—down the side of the house with his tall, muscular body. His biceps were bigger than my thighs, and one strained when he pointed somewhere. Then I heard his deep, rough, almost growly voice, "Put it down over there. Gonna build a shed soon."

I knew then that the person who'd moved in was the tall, well-built, dark-haired man with a hard gaze.

With a glance behind me to the stairs, I wondered if I called for help, would he come to my rescue?

I could be free from my hellhole, or was it yet another risk I couldn't take for Harriet's sake?

All I had to do was open my mouth and shout out.

Looking back outside, my gaze landed on some children running into the backyard. Were those his children? Did he have a wife? A girlfriend? Why did it feel like my stomach bottomed out with that thought?

My door swung open. I flew down to sit on the cot and curled my knees up, my arms around them. I flicked my eyes to the small bathroom in the corner. I should have made a run for it and locked myself in there.

Gloria came down the stairs, her hair a mess and make-up from the night before smeared over her face.

My breath caught at the sight of the blade in her hands.

She hadn't cut me since that night. Why did she hold it once again?

"Gloria—"

"Shut the fuck up," she snapped low. She came at me, her blade touched my neck, her hand gripped my hair. She pulled me up and moved me to look out the window. "Know you heard someone moving in. You even think to shout, to call for help, you know what will happen to not only you but your old friend."

"Y-you won't get your money," I told her bravely, if only my voice didn't shake.

She laughed, not even surprised I knew her play. "I won't care. You'll be out of my hair." The knife dug deeper into my neck. "But you want to get smart. Look out there." When I didn't, she shook my head by my hair. "Look. See those kids, the women, the men?" I didn't reply. She went on. "Yeah, you see them. Then you know if you get any type of attention from any of them, it won't be you and your friend's lives lost. It'll be theirs." My pulse raced. "You know what Lenny brought home last night? A gun, Emerson. A gun can do a lot more damage than this fucking knife. It can kill a lot more than *one* person. You do anything, their lives are on your hands like the others. Got me?"

"Yes," I whispered.

She shoved me forwards, and I landed hard on my knees on the concrete floor. My upper body slumped over the bed. I sucked in a shaky breath, and tears trailed down my cheeks. I listened to her storm away, knowing she knew she had me.

Knew I wouldn't do anything to risk other people. Especially children.

She'd always said my heart was too soft. She couldn't understand why I mourned my dad for so long. Even called me weak for it. Only I knew Gloria didn't have a good bone in her body. She would never understand how much it could crush a person when you lost someone you loved.

I couldn't let anyone else feel that loss.

No one else would die for me.

No one would know anything.

I would keep my mouth closed.

Stupidly, once more, I found myself praying for a miracle.

CHAPTER FOUR

EMERSON

*R*yan Warden had been officially moved in for a week now. I remembered the woman calling him Ryan, and her man not liking it. It seemed all the others called him by his last name. Though I wasn't sure if it was his last name and not a nickname. Either way, I liked his name.

It was strong, like him.

His place had many visitors over the week. Men, big scary men, and women who smiled and laughed a lot. I wanted to know what made them so happy in life, because I would love it for myself one day.

Yes, I still held out hope. Stupidly.

The door to my room opened. I quickly sat on the bed and waited. It would be a meal delivery—I got two a day. Thankfully, they were big meals, so I kept what I could in case I annoyed them enough to get nothing one day.

Gloria glared at me, dumped the tray on the small table near the bottom of the stairs, and stomped back up, leaving without saying a word.

I preferred those days. It was better than being yelled at, stomped, or spat on.

She'd already inflicted enough scars. I didn't need more.

Glancing down at my arms, I traced a finger over the jagged lines. Tears welled, but I quickly wiped them away.

I didn't know what I did to deserve a life living with two monsters. Hadn't God already taken enough from me? But he seemed to want more and more. Why else would I have to stay locked up with Gloria and Lenny? Though, I hardly saw Lenny anymore. The only times I did was when Gloria had to go out for some reason. He must have been effectively reprimanded by Gloria because he kept to himself when he entered. But his eyes still held something in them I didn't like.

"Warden, gotta head out" I heard called. I spun, got to my knees, and then stood on the bed. It was the biker with dark hair and a scowl. I was sure his name was Talon.

All men called Ryan "Warden," but I couldn't seem to bring myself to do it. I liked the name Ryan for him. Maybe it was because it softened him a little compared to his rough look and large body.

Ryan came into view when he replied, "All good, brother. Thanks for the hand." They did some type of handshake, and Talon left. Warden looked back to the garden shed they'd been building for the last two days.

It had been a sight to watch them.

A very nice sight.

My eyes seemed to like watching Ryan.

A lot.

I didn't understand the attraction, why him more than others. Why would I feel interested in a male after being treated the way I had been by Lenny?

I didn't have an answer; all I knew was how my attention always swung to Ryan.

He stood in the yard, hands on his hips, sweaty, dirty, and yet he still caused my heart to beat faster.

Never had I had this type of reaction for a man, until then.

Living next door to Ryan gave me a form of entertainment besides the ratty books that I'd read over and over, piled behind some of the boxes. Safely hidden from Gloria. I had no doubt she'd get rid of them if she knew I liked them. It would be something she'd do.

Ryan turned. He dragged out his phone from the back pocket of his snuggly fit jeans and did something on there as he made his way to the back deck, up onto it, before disappearing inside.

Disappointment washed over me.

Then guilt reared its ugly mug, telling me I should have felt the same attraction to Donny that I did for Ryan. Maybe then I would have saved him. If only I'd cared more.

Shit, could I have…? Fuck. No. I couldn't think like that.

While guilt lived inside of me, I wouldn't allow it to control my thoughts in that way.

Sitting back down on the bed, I pulled the notebook out from under the duffle coat I used as a pillow. Flipping it open, I stared down at my drawing. Art had never been a subject I liked, but over the past couple of years, I had tried to draw what the other men looked like in the room that night.

I wasn't the best artist, but time had given me the gift to work on the pictures, and I was sure I had them near perfect.

The boss had blond hair, blue eyes. A jaw that sat a little crooked, a long, slim nose, and bushy brows. The rapist had long, light brown hair. His nose was thicker, his eyes darker, his jaw straight, but a scar ran from the tip of his chin down his neck.

I hadn't thought I'd remember them so clearly after everything.

My mind should have shredded the memory of that night, but it hadn't. I met that night over and over in my dreams. I pictured them perfectly in my nightmares.

In the hope that one day my drawings would help someone.

If they didn't kill me first.

What I couldn't remember was what the girl looked like. I hardly saw her face—just a glimpse of red hair, a side profile of pale skin, a splatter of freckles over her cheek.

That was when my dreams screwed with me, because in them, I was that girl on the couch. Then on other nights, I was Donny being shot in the head.

They happened so often that I tried not to sleep. Even after two years. I'd thought they'd lessen somewhat, but they hadn't. Maybe it had something to do with still being trapped. Still feeling alone. Forgotten. Or maybe I just couldn't forget—and, in a way, I didn't want to.

Naturally, the tragedies would plague me in the waking *and* sleeping hours. As they should. Donny deserved to be remembered, as did Mrs Minna, and even the young girl. Yes, I knew they had family to mourn them also, but I'd been there. I'd been through it with them. They died because of me, so it was my sin to remember, to keep living and feeling the event of their deaths, their pain.

Sniffing, I put the notebook aside and got up from the bed to stretch. I walked over to the toilet room. That was where I was soaking the sleeves I'd torn up to use as a pad for when that time of the month kicked me in the guts. I had to be inventive for a lot of things. For the cold nights where I had no socks to wear, I found a pair of long woollen gloves in a box and used those, washing them when the days were warmer and I hadn't needed them. For blankets, I had a thin one and used the extra clothes I'd found. Some jackets, hoodies, even a long winter coat that looked like it came from the seventies based on the multicolours over it.

I wasn't sure where or who the clothes belonged to. I couldn't see Gloria or Lenny ever having worn them. However, it didn't matter. I needed them. Even if they smelled of mothballs.

After wringing out the sleeves, I took them into the basement and hung them over boxes. It would take a while to air dry them, having to flip them over and over, but they'd get there. They were stained, of course, but using them again and again was better than ruining my only pair of underwear. Underwear that nearly dropped off when I wasn't wearing pants, jeans, or shorts. I'd lost a lot of weight. Too much. But I couldn't do anything about it.

My head dropped forwards, chin nearly hitting my chest.

My fucking life was devastating.

What was I honestly waiting for? To turn twenty-five and then be killed once they got my inheritance? Why didn't they forge my signature? Why didn't they get me to sign something now and then kill me? Why wait? Unless they liked the torture. Or maybe the lawyer or whoever was in charge of the inheritance needed to see me in person to sign it over?

If that was the case, would that be my chance of escape?

A fire lit inside my chest. Stupid hope played with me once more.

But if they did have to take me out of the house, I might have a chance to do something to get away from them. Then I would race to Harriet's, to save her before saving myself and calling the police to ruin Gloria.

The new fire spread throughout my body. I felt giddy. A small laugh fell from my lips, so I slapped my hand over my mouth. With wide eyes, I tilted my head to the side and listened. No one approached.

Did I honestly dare to hope I could escape them?

Then again, what was wrong with hoping? It gave me a new strength.

Since I was nineteen, I had six more years to put up with what I was.

Six more years.

Could I do it?

I glanced at the bed, the notepad.

I would try.

God, I wanted to, because it meant I might live. Live and be lucky enough to have found some type of happiness. Maybe even a happiness like I'd seen in the women who visited next door. A life around people who cared.

When I heard a noise from next door, I rushed over to the window, hopped up to stand on the bed, and looked out.

Ryan stood on the back deck with a beer bottle in hand. He'd taken a shower; his hair still glistened from the water. I watched as he lifted the bottle to his lips and took a long drink.

Why did I suddenly wish I were that beer bottle?

That was a strange thing to think.

I bit my bottom lip to stop myself from smiling at the silly thought.

His hand dropped. He gripped the bottle by the rim of it and took a couple of steps to the table on his deck. After he placed the bottle down, he pulled out his phone again.

After a couple of seconds, he was smiling.

That was a rarity. He tended to only smile around one woman. The one who was taken by the man called Declan.

I liked his smile. Even my belly liked it, because it twisted in a way that thrilled me.

Was it her on the phone? Had she texted him? Told him she wanted him? I shook my head at the foolishness. She wouldn't do that to Declan. Even I could see the love they had for one another when I saw them at Ryan's.

So then what was he smiling at on the phone?

I wondered if I could ever make him or any man smile like that.

I slid my hand to my neck and brushed against my hair. I glanced down and picked up a part of my long, greasy dark locks. Only the scars on my arm caught my attention. I slumped down to the bed, leaning my back against the wall.

No one would want me.

If I ever got free, Gloria made sure no one would want me.

How could they? I had scars on the inside and out.

I was dirty, even though I washed every day.

Dirty in ways a man couldn't trust and love.

Dragging my legs up, knees to my chest, I wrapped my arms around them and dropped my head to my knees.

What did I have if I got free?

Nothing.

Nothing but my life.

Could I make something of it?

I didn't know.

People were cruel. And I wasn't talking about monsters like Gloria and Lenny. People could be vicious with words, with looks…. They'd look at me, but what would they see? A broken woman, or one who was trying to be brave and live on?

Then again, even if I became a lonely lady with a billion cats, it would be worth it because it meant I would be free.

CHAPTER FIVE

EMERSON

*A*nother few days went by and Ryan hadn't been around much. He had to have been working. I wouldn't mind knowing what he did for a living. It had to be something to do with heavy lifting. Early one morning, I had the pleasure of watching him out on his deck in only tracksuit pants doing sit-ups and press-ups.

Yes, I'd seen guys work out before, but Ryan Warden working out could be a new TV show every woman would watch.

Thinking of it now, while I ate my dinner meal of mash and some type of funny-looking meat, it would be good of Ryan if he did his show every morning. At least one viewing seemed to keep my mind active for a couple of days. I couldn't wait for a repeat though.

Did that make me a stalker? A pervert? Maybe both, which in a way made me feel a bit sick about it. Right, from that day on, I would stop watching Ryan so much.

At least I'd try.

I'd also rip up the paper I had his phone number on. Earlier in the day, he'd been sitting drinking a coffee on his deck, talking on the phone about some drywall order. He told them his number, and while I'd been gripping my notebook to my chest, because I'd been writing, I quickly jotted it down. I didn't know why or what I'd do with it, but my hand took action before my brain caught up with it.

My attention on Ryan was becoming too much. Yes, I really had to stop. Especially when I knew nothing could come from it.

But then I heard his back door swing open with a bang through my already-open window.

"This is nice," someone said loudly, and I was sure it was a female voice.

A woman.

Was it the woman who'd been with Declan?

Ryan's friend?

Pushing my dish aside, I climbed to my feet on the bed and glanced out, frowning when I saw it wasn't his friend. Instead, it was a woman I hadn't seen around Ryan before, and the way she looked at him twisted my stomach.

Was it sane to hate a person I'd never met?

"Yeah, I like it," Ryan replied. He took a sip from the glass he held in his hand. It was dark outside, but a light from inside his house shined out onto the back deck. I could see the liquid in the glass was either dark brown or black.

The woman held her own glass with the same coloured liquor—I doubted they'd be drinking cordial.

"How long you been here?" she asked. Obviously she didn't know Ryan well. So why were they together now?

"Few weeks," he said, voice low and rough. A voice I wanted talking to me. Eyes I wanted looking over my body like he was hers.

Until I remembered I was nothing like her. She was big

busted, with long legs, blonde hair, short skirt, tight top. I had visible scars, long dark hair, and dark eyes. Not only that, I was short and skinny like a starved greyhound.

Was I jealous?

How could I be jealous?

Ryan was good-looking, but I didn't actually feel things for him. That would be weird.

I didn't.

The guy was practically a stranger.

A headache suddenly throbbed at my temples. Finally, after years in a small, damp basement, I was losing it. Losing it enough to gain some type of feelings for a man I didn't know. An older man.

No. I wasn't jealous. I wouldn't let myself be.

"You wanna hit the restaurant?" Ryan asked. He was taking *her* out on a date.

Closing my eyes, I rested my head on the ledge. A vision of pulling her hair so she'd get away from him popped into my mind. "Don't be stupid, Emerson," I muttered to myself.

I glanced back out, covered my mouth with my hand, and bounced down to sit on the bed. Ryan had been looking this way. He wouldn't have seen me. He shouldn't have. The window was tiny, it was dark, and the wire fence would have obscured the top of my head and eyes.

Moving my hand, I took a deep breath to calm my erratic heart. I tilted my head, straining my ears to hear anything. They were talking. If I wanted to hear what was being said, I needed to get closer.

Slowly, I got to my shaky legs and straightened. With my back to the wall, I stood beside the window and rested my head close to the opening. Their voices became clear.

"I didn't hear anything," she said.

"Hmm," Ryan grunted.

"Hey." Her voice changed—it went lower, sweeter. "How about we have dessert before dinner?"

Ryan chuckled. "You'd want that?"

"Yeah, baby. I'd definitely want that."

I ground my teeth together. She wasn't really talking about what I thought she was. She couldn't be.

Taking a chance, I sneakily peeked out the window. My eyes widened when I spotted Ryan reaching out, grabbing the woman's arm and hauling her into him. Their mouths collided. She moaned, and then again when Ryan picked her up to plant her bottom on the outdoor table.

She ate his face while his hand slid under her skirt.

I wanted to yell at him that he didn't know where she'd been or cause some loud noise to scare them into stopping.

He deserved better. Someone who dressed nice. Who would go to dinner before having dessert…. Then again, he wasn't complaining.

Then it clicked.

This was what a one-night stand would be like.

Maybe I was simply hoping it would be because I really didn't like her for him. She kissed weird, nearly licked his face off. Her nails were like claws as she ran them up and down his back.

My breath caught when I saw Ryan tug her panties from her body. "You wet, sugar?" he demanded in a coarse, totally turned-on tone.

"God, yes," she panted.

I had to look away, but then she grabbed his tee and said, "No need to prep, baby. I'm ready."

What did that mean?

Prep what?

If my heart didn't stop beating so hard that it rang in my ears, I was about to carve it out of my body with a blunt pencil.

"You sure?"

"Oh yeah. I was wet when I first saw you. Wetter now feeling you."

I didn't need to hear that. I screwed my nose up and clenched my teeth. I also felt like banging my head against the bricks.

Ryan's hand disappeared between them. Was he touching her?

The woman smiled. "Told you."

Ryan growled low, causing my heart to beat harder. He grabbed something out of his wallet from his back pocket, then threw it to the floor. His hand went back between them for a moment longer, and he thrust his hips forwards. She moaned for a long time. Ryan groaned in the back of his throat, and then they were at each other with hands, lips, and teeth.

It was then I realised he was fucking her.

"Harder," she cried.

My eyes were transfixed on his hips. In and out they went, over and over.

My belly fluttered, something clenched lower, and I figured out what she meant by wet when I suddenly felt my panties dampen.

I needed to look away.

Stop watching.

It was wrong.

So very wrong.

But I couldn't stop watching his hips, how he ground into her and then slid back out to then do it again.

My clit throbbed. It had never done that. Not even before when I touched myself.

Why was it throbbing at the sight of Ryan fucking?

While I understood why people watched porn and got off on it, everything about this moment and my whole situation was wrong in every possible way. Getting turned on in the here and now sent my mind spinning. What the hell was wrong with me?

The woman moaned and cried out like she was a porn star. Not that I'd seen any, but I'd heard others talk about it. Her noises annoyed me. If I were her, I would be quieter. I'd be kissing him a lot more. I would want him naked so I could touch him everywhere I could.

My mouth dried.

I wanted to be her.

I wanted Ryan fucking me.

In all different ways.

If it didn't skeeve me completely, I would have reached into my panties and touched myself, but I couldn't bring myself to. It felt wrong.

Instead, I sank to my knees, hand on my thigh, gripping, and breathing deeply. Trying to calm down. I was disgusted at myself for watching. That was private. I shouldn't have done that. I was revolted with myself for liking it, for wanting it to be me Ryan was all over, for feeling not only my clit throb but lower. Where I wanted him planted inside of me.

The woman's cry of pleasure hit my ears. It was loud. Not wanting to hear how Ryan sounded after he came, I curled down onto the bed and pulled the coat over my head. My mind conjured up the thought of me in the woman's position, but I pushed it away and started counting.

From that moment and on, I knew the thought of keeping my attention off Ryan wouldn't only be a thought. I had to make it an action, or my sick fascination would turn into something bad. There was no way in hell I would become any type of monster like Gloria.

I was probably being far-fetched, over-imagining what could happen if I kept watching Ryan, but I wouldn't chance it.

He would exist next door, but I had to curb my curiosity.

I'd continue my days as if Ryan Warden hadn't moved in.

I would spend my boring existence reading the books I'd read over and over for the last couple of years. I would draw, write, clean, exercise, and try to survive until I had a chance to get away.

If I got that chance.

No, I would.

Like Lenny had said, they wanted my money. I had to believe they would keep me alive for me to sign it over personally or else they would have gotten rid of me a long time ago. I had to believe that with every breath I took.

CHAPTER SIX

EMERSON

*T*he most beautiful thing happened about a month later. I'd kept to my promise; I only watched out the window when I knew Ryan would be at work. I didn't know what he did with his nights or early mornings. If he worked out or didn't.

It was late, so late the moon was shining brightly high in the sky. I'd woken from a nightmare sweaty, shaky, and with a hammering heart. Then I heard it. At first, it was just a guitar softly playing. I knew it wasn't the music Gloria or Lenny listened to because that was heavy and pounding.

This was beautiful.

Rubbing a hand over my face, I got out of bed, seeing enough around me from the light in the toilet room I always left on, with the door just about closed so no light would reach the window. As soon as I moved away from my bed, the music sounded softer. I glanced back to the window. Was Ryan playing music? I went back over to the bed. Since it was a warm night, the window was still open. I climbed up next to it, leaning against the wall.

The soft strum of the strings of the guitar was magical.

I hadn't heard beauty in such a long time.

What made it more magical was the voice that started singing with the tunes.

Ryan's deep baritone, along with the guitar, caused me to grip my tee at my chest. Tears sprang quickly to my eyes and flowed over, running a trail down my cheeks.

Turning, I flattened myself against the brick wall, my cheek pressed against it, and I couldn't help but reach my hand up, fingers touching the window ledge. I wanted to get close, to wrap my whole body in his music. I didn't know if it was a well-known song or one he'd made up himself; whatever it was, I loved it.

It was something I needed in my life. A sense of softness, of something tender reaching into my chest and lighting it with life.

I rolled my head, resting my forehead against the brick. I flattened my other hand against the wall. Listening, feeling, and crying quietly over the wonder.

When the song ended and he started with another, I stayed right where I was, never wanting to miss something that warmed me throughout. Ryan didn't know, but he was sharing a breathtaking treat with me, and I would always treasure it.

As he started another, one I actually knew, I hummed quietly along with it.

My dad and I loved music. There wasn't a day that went by where we didn't have a record, CD, or radio playing in the background.

One day I'd pestered him to get with the times and buy a Bluetooth speaker we could connect our phones to. His reply had been "Emmie, we don't need to waste money on some babytooth speaker or whatever it is. We have my stereo and the radios. We have all we need for the two of us." And we had.

We worked, ate, and cleaned along with music day in and out. We tried singing along with the songs, but both Dad and I had terrible voices. Music connected my memories to many good times.

I covered my mouth as a sob caught in my throat. I missed my dad. Missed my old friends from my other school. Missed the farm. Missed the animals. Missed my freedom.

Ryan moved on to another song, his fingers drifting over the strings with ease. Why was he awake so late? Did he have trouble sleeping?

Suddenly, he stopped playing. My heart cracked. I needed more, wanted more. Without really thinking, I flew off the bed, across the room, and pulled out my phone from its hiding place. I opened the message box, and using the anonymous texting app, which sends a different, untraceable number than the one assigned to my phone, I typed out **Please play more.** I hit Send to the only number I had stored in my phone. Why I stored it, I didn't know, because I had ripped the paper up with his number on it and flushed it away.

My heart crept up my throat, thickening it.

I'd sent a message to Ryan.

I'd sent it because I needed more beauty in my life.

Because hearing him play reminded me of some good times I'd had.

Good times where I'd been loved, safe, and happy.

I fumbled with the phone when it vibrated in my hand.

Licking my dry lips, I then bit my bottom one. Could I open it? I wasn't sure if I should.

My pulse ticked hard in my throat; my head pounded from anxiety.

With a shaky hand, I pressed the button to light it up. He replied, **Who's this?**

I wiped at the sweat beading over my upper lip. Nerves

pulled at my stomach. Still, I tapped out a response. **Someone who needs music right now.**

I pressed Send and regretted it right away. Would he think I wanted him to play all night?

The phone buzzed. Since I just programmed his name in, the new message popped up with **Ryan: You live around here?**

Unknown: Yes.

Ryan: Where?

Ignoring the question, I asked again. **Unknown: Just one more song. Please.**

He didn't reply. Hanging my head, I closed my eyes and clenched my phone to my chest. But then I heard it. I slapped a hand over my mouth and raced back over to the bed. I climbed on it and stood next to the window.

Ryan's voice mixed with the beat wonderfully. It was a country song, and I loved it more than any of the others because now I knew he was doing it for me, only he didn't know who I was. But I didn't care about that fact.

I stared out into the night sky and listened to a song about a woman being beautifully crazy. It was the best moment I'd had in years. My chest expanded with how much I felt right then.

I wanted to be that woman in the song.

A combination of happy and sad tears flowed down. While it was amazing to listen to, I wanted nothing more than for Ryan to actually be singing it to me.

Me.

The scarred, marked, dirty woman.

When it came to an end, I wanted to ask him to sing it again and again.

Ryan: There. The one more song.

My smile was the biggest it had ever been in ages.

Unknown: Thank you. So much.

Ryan: Why did you need it?

Unknown: You play wonderfully, and your voice is... soothing.

Wanting to know if he was outside texting or inside, I had to look. I'd kick myself later for the moment of weakness.

Gripping the window ledge with my fingers, I leaned over to glance out. He stood in nothing but jeans on the deck with his hands on his hips, looking around at the houses in his neighbourhood.

Little did he know I was right next door looking out at him.

Ryan ran a hand through his hair and raised the other near his chest, which held his phone in it.

Ryan: You need help?

He didn't know, but right then I knew he was a good man. A man who didn't deserve a burden like me.

Unknown: No. Sorry to disturb you.

Ryan: How'd you get this number?

Unknown: Magic. Going to sleep now.

I looked over to see him read the text, glance around, and then drop his arm to his side. He sighed. When he turned, I got a quick view of his face before he went through the back door with a slam. His brows were drawn; he looked concerned and annoyed. He probably thought he'd find me standing at the end of his bed holding an axe or something just as crazy.

God, what have I done?

Unknown: I promise I won't be trouble. It was the right thing to do. I didn't want him worried.

When no answer came, I guessed he was probably getting ready for bed. Brushing his teeth... something I hadn't done for a long time. I washed them with water, used material to clean them as much as I could. Or Ryan could be taking a shower, another thing I wished I could do. Water from a sink only did so much. I still felt disgusting every day.

I dropped to the bed, opened the screen to look at his messages. I ran my fingers over them, smiling to myself. I spoke to someone out in the real world.

A crazy conversation, but still one nonetheless. Even though it was small, it was something to me. So was him singing. I pressed two fingers against my lips to stop myself from laughing giddily.

I would cherish this night for the rest of my life.

Ryan didn't know, but he'd given me a gift.

I nearly squealed when my phone vibrated.

I scrolled down to the bottom and read his words.

Ryan: Guess I'll see.

He would.

Unknown: You will.

Ryan: What's your name?

My heart jumped hard. I couldn't give him my name. Could I? No, if he searched anything about me, he would see a police report from whatever Gloria had told them. If he was smart, and he looked it, then he would know I was in the house. Never would I risk him or anyone else.

Although, maybe I could at least give him a part of it. **Emmie.** I quickly added so I didn't look as if I already knew it: **Yours?**

Ryan: Warden.

He'd given me his last name, but I didn't mind. He was still talking, so I would go with it.

Emmie: Thank you again, Warden.

Ryan: How old are you?

Damn, what would look okay in his eyes? I didn't think he'd continue texting a nineteen-year-old. He seemed in his late thirties; at least, I thought he was.

Emmie: Why?

Ryan: Need to know I'm not texting some kid.

I wasn't a child, even if he thought a teen was still classed as a kid. My dad had always told me I was old for my actual age, and I was sure over the last two years I'd aged even more. **Thirty.** It was the best age I could think of at that moment.

Ryan: Why're you up late?

Emmie: Why are you?

Ryan: Couldn't sleep.

I smiled.

Emmie: Me neither.

Ryan: Better try and get some. Night, Emmie.

My whole body warmed.

Emmie: Night, Warden.

I lay back, crushing the phone to my chest. This was dangerous. I shouldn't have messaged him. He'd already been my object of attention and now he had me feeling... euphoric. An intense happiness. It scared me.

However, I had managed to stop watching him.

Only I had a feeling that would be blown out of the water. I wanted to see him, watch him. See his mouth move and imagine he'd sing just for me. Sighing, I sat up. I needed to hide the phone in case Gloria or Lenny came down while I slept and found it. I quickly hid it and did something silly. Humming the song, I danced over to the bed.

Laughing softly, I lay back down and flicked the jacket over me. I tucked another jacket under my head and closed my eyes. A smile picked up my lips in the dark because in my mind, I could still hear his voice singing that one song. A song I would listen to on repeat if it was Ryan singing it.

It was the best way to fall asleep.

CHAPTER SEVEN

WARDEN

*S*itting at my desk at work, I glanced down to my phone once again. My mind was on the texts I'd gotten the night before. It was fucking strange. Someone in my damn new neighbourhood listened to me. I'd thought, since it was the middle of the damn night, no one else would have been awake, but I'd been wrong. Never had anyone heard me play and sing; it was something I kept to myself. I only did it when I couldn't sleep, usually because a case wasn't coming together.

The first text shocked the shit out of me. I would have stopped playing, but when I'd asked why she wanted me to sing another and she answered, it gripped at something inside of me.

She felt soothed by my voice.

It seemed she really needed it though. I got that from the few texts.

Emmie.

Cute name.

But was it her real one?

That was the problem. I didn't think it was, because when I got into work, I looked up the people around my house and didn't find anyone by the name of Emmie.

Where was she, then?

I goddamn hated puzzles because I wanted to solve them. Yet I had a feeling I needed or wanted to take my time with this one. I had to find out more about the woman.

Picking up my phone, I shot off, **What're you doing?**

There wasn't an answer right away or even an hour later. I bloody checked again and again. Maybe she worked and couldn't reply.

"Hey, Warden, did you get the fax from Tom yet?" Violet asked. She was my boss, but she treated her employees like we were all on the same level. Didn't think I would work for a woman in a private investigating office, yet there I was. I'd started out life in the army, fucking hated it. So I saved, delisted, and got my degree in criminal justice with a certificate in security operations and investigative services. Worked for a joint in Melbourne. Couldn't stand the owner—he thought his shit didn't stink. I moved to the country, was going to take a bouncer job until, to my goddamn shock, I saw an ad for an investigator. Didn't think a small town would need a firm, but after being around for four years, I knew Violet had a name for herself. Clients came from all around Australia asking for help. Though, since Violet had gotten back into the fold with her brother, the local president of the Hawks MC, it seemed our time got even busier, as well as our usual workload.

"Not yet," I called.

I heard her chair squeak and looked over to see her leaning back in it with her eyes on me. "You checked recently? Because I haven't seen you check anything but your phone for the last hour."

Shit.

"Nope," I said, then rolled my chair back to check the fax machine. Fucking hell, it was sitting there, and it said he'd sent it an hour ago.

"You good?"

"Yep." I read over the file, knowing Violet was still looking at me. Thank Christ, Tom sent me something I could follow up. Standing, I pocketed my phone. I grabbed my gun from my locked drawer and slipped it into the back of my jeans. I'd fucking forgotten my holster in the car. "Gonna run out. Tom got the report in from toxicology. She had been doped up to the max. Headin' to the club she was last at. Asked about her, but never questioned them about drugs happenin' in the area."

Violet shot me a chin lift. "Keep your head in the game." Yeah, she knew my mind was elsewhere that morning.

"Will do. When Zara gets back, tell her to keep my lunch warm in the oven."

She snorted. "Can't have your precious lunch go to waste."

Narrowing my eyes, I told her, "Not when it's from Seymore's. And if you or Butch fuckin' even think of eatin' it, I'll kill you."

"You threaten, and yet it never happens."

"It will this day."

She waved me off and went back to whatever she'd been doing on the computer. I made my way out to my Hilux ute. The mother of the girl who'd been at the club even when she was underage had contacted Vi's office to look into it. She felt the cops weren't doing enough, and she wanted the men to pay for what they'd done to her girl. Not only had she been drugged, but they raped her, then dumped her body in a back alley. It'd been the previous night I'd found out her case wasn't the only one, and this shit had been going on for fucking years. It was no wonder the mum, Mrs Henson, felt the cops wouldn't get the answers she wanted. I just damn hoped I could get them for her.

The club wasn't far. I knew it'd be open because during the day, people could get pub meals there. Walking in, I headed straight to the bar. Two barmen were behind the counter. One was taking meal orders, the other drinks. Since I wasn't eating, I waited for the other.

When he made his way towards me, I took in his name tag. Terry.

He nodded. "Hey, man. What can I get you?"

"Name's Warden. I work for an investigation firm. Hired by the mother of the young girl who got taken from here over a month ago. Know the police have gone through the videos, interviewed people. What I want to know is if anyone workin' here knows about the high percentage of drugs in the area."

"Look, man, you're asking the wrong person. I only work the day shift, and I can honestly say I haven't seen any dealings here. The man you need is the manager. He can get you a list of the night staff. They're the better ones to question."

"Okay, where can I find the manager?"

"He's on holidays for another two weeks."

Fucking hell.

"Then who's in charge until he gets back?"

"Phillip at the register there. But he's a lazy fuck. Made sure he only works days, never comes in at night. That's what I heard from Shanti."

Goddamn idiots.

"Who's Shanti?"

"Oh, a girl who works night shifts that I'm screwing. Shanti Summers."

"You got a number for her?"

"Yeah, sure." He grabbed his phone out and rattled off the

number. I quickly jotted it down. "Do you want me to tell her you're wanting to talk to her?"

"No. In fact, don't tell anyone we spoke."

His brows dipped. "Looks kinda suss we've been speaking this whole time."

"If anyone asks, think of somethin' to say. If I find out Shanti or anyone on night shift is expectin' me, I'll know you talked, and I won't be fuckin' pleased. Get me, Terry?"

"Yes," he just about squeaked.

With a chin lift, I turned and walked out of the bar, back into the cool air. I pressed a number into my phone. Butch answered, "Yeah?"

"Need an address, a Shanti Summers."

"On it. Oh, and thanks for lunch."

"You fucker," I got out to a laughing Butch before he hung up. The guy hadn't been on the team long at Violet's firm, but he was solid. It was a sad day when Chuck left, but having Butch as his replacement was good.

When my phone rang again, I expected it to be Butch. "What?"

"Someone's in a mood." I could hear the smile in Mally's voice.

Malinda May, or Mally as a lot of people called her, was a woman I could have fucking fallen for. That was if she ever looked past Declan Stoke, a member of the Hawks MC. Now she had her happy ever after with a man who thought she was the shit. Which she was. Sweet, caring, calm, happy, and damn beautiful.

She'd had some shit happen about a year ago. Violet helped out, which had me helping also. Mally and I got close. Not the close I wanted, but having her as a friend meant a ton to me than not having her in my life.

"Darlin', how you doin'?"

"Good. But I'm guessing your day could be better."

"It is now." I grinned when I heard her laugh. "What can I do for you?"

"Josh has been hounding me to ring you. He wants to know if he can come stay at your place over the weekend."

"The boy should ring himself and ask."

"I told him that. I think no matter how much he looks up to you, you still intimidate him a little."

"Me? He lives with a badarse and I intimidate him?"

"I know. I can't explain the mind of a fifteen-year-old."

"You tell him when he calls, I'll let him know the answer. As long as you and Stoke are cool with it."

"You know we are."

"Even Stoke?"

She laughed. "Yes. He might not like our friendship, but he understands it. He trusts you, Ryan. With me, and with the kids."

"Good. Get your kid to call me."

"Will do. Lastly, when are you coming for dinner?" Hanging out with them separately I could deal with, but after the last dinner I went to the other night left me feeling like I was missing out on something in my life, I stayed away. I didn't like it.

"After I have a house-warming."

She sighed. "You've been saying you're going to have one, but it hasn't happened."

Wasn't sure if it would happen, which was why I used it as an excuse for not going to dinner, for now. Soon I'd have to think of something else, or Mally would sniff out the problem. Then she'd try and set me up with someone. I didn't want that shit. I was good with fucking and leaving, or me getting them out of my house.

"Know that, darlin', but one day I will."

"Fine. We'll talk soon."

"You got it. Later."

"Bye, Ryan."

Stoke was one fucking lucky man.

Shaking my head, I pocketed my phone and climbed in my ute. I decided to head to the office, see if Butch had taken my lunch, beat the shit out of him if he had, while waiting on details of that Shanti bird.

It wasn't until I pulled up out the front that my phone pinged. Taking it out, I saw I had a message waiting for me from an unknown number. I glanced down at my chest, wondering why my fucking heart acted weird. Ignoring it, I opened the message.

Emmie: Sorry for the late response, I was working.

Why did it feel like a lie?

Ryan: What do you do?

Emmie: Stuff. You?

Ryan: Stuff.

An uneasy feeling settled in my gut. She didn't want to say much about herself, and it told me she was either a fake, some kid messing with me, or she had troubles.

From the messages before, I was definitely leaning towards troubles.

However, if I found out it was a kid, I'd teach them not to mess with anyone again.

Christ. I scrubbed a hand over my face as my phone beeped. Why was I not wanting it to be a kid? Jesus, was I that desperate for a woman's attention that I was going to continue this shit?

Fuck no. I wasn't desperate. I could find a woman to warm my dick if needed.

Like I'd felt before, I needed to know where this was going. Who Emmie was and if she needed help. Why else would she text some guy in the middle of the night needing more music in her life?

Emmie: I'm sorry. I'm boring. My job isn't worth talking about. I shouldn't have texted in the first place.

Ryan: You never did say how you got my number.

Emmie: I did. I said magic.

Ryan: Right. Forgot it. Just need to know, darlin', do you need help?

There wasn't a reply for a good few minutes. I watched the clock.

Emmie: Why would you ask?

Ryan: Not many would message a stranger in the middle of the night asking for another song because it was soothing to them.

Another couple of minutes passed.

Emmie: I had a nightmare. Your music helped.

What made her have bad dreams?

She sent another, and it fucking annoyed me.

Emmie: I'm going to stop messaging you. I shouldn't have started. I'm sorry.

She wanted to run because I'd asked too many questions. I just knew it.

I'd let her think she'd won, until later when I wasn't supposed to be working and was at home. Until then, I'd shove it to the back of my mind and get on with my day. Or damn well try to.

CHAPTER EIGHT

EMERSON

$\mathcal{I}$ slept through the morning since I didn't get much the night before. What scared me was how I hadn't woken when either Lenny or Gloria delivered my lunch. When I opened my eyes, I saw it sitting on the floor at the end of the stairs. Only the fear evaporated when my thoughts drifted to the previous night.

Ryan Warden.

His voice, the way he easily played the guitar. Both mixed together amazingly.

With excitement rolling through my belly, I made my way over to my hiding spot for my phone. While I ate, I wanted to read through the texts again. Only when I pulled it free, I saw I had a text waiting for me.

Ryan had reached out to me.

He texted me first on a new day.

My hands shook as my excitement bubbled up higher. I opened the message… and my smile slipped from my lips.

He'd asked what I was doing.

What could I tell him? *Living in a basement because my aunt wants to keep me locked away after I saw something I wished I never had? Oh, and they killed two people because of me, but hey, that's okay. I'm sure I won't get you killed.*

No.

I had to lie, lie, lie, and I hated myself for it, but if it meant keeping him safe, I would.

When I sent back an apology with my delay and how I was busy with work, I regretted it as soon as I pressed the button. It was too late to take it back though, and I was surprised with how quickly he replied asking what work I did.

I thought responding with "stuff" would get me out of it, especially when I asked what he did. But when his short same-word reply came back, I hated it. He was being evasive because I was.

Before I would say anything, not that I knew what to say even when sorry didn't feel enough, he asked me how I got his number. He mustn't have reread the messages like I had the night before, because I certainly remembered telling him. So I said that.

Ryan: Right. Forgot it. Just need to know, darlin', do you need help?

My heart stumbled over its next beat. Darlin'. It wasn't darling, but darlin'.

"Darlin'," I tried aloud. A new smile touched my lips and tugged up the corners. I read the text again, puzzled as to why he would ask if I needed help. Which was what I sent back.

Ryan: Not many would message a stranger in the middle of the night asking for another song because it was soothing to them.

That was true. It had been crazy for me to do it. But he gave me something I wouldn't forget, so I replied with the truth, about waking from a nightmare and how his music helped me. A tightness in my chest formed after I sent it. Regret.

Reaching out to him and the continuing messaging wasn't going to work. I didn't know the man, even when he seemed like a good person. I had to put a stop to it.

I had to.

For my sake and especially his.

Which had me replying with how I was going to stop messaging him, and I shouldn't have done it in the first place. How I was sorry.

I had been sorry. For annoying his life, for not having him in mine, for thinking I could continue whatever this was... a budding friendship, with attraction on my part for him. Still, it would end.

It had to.

I just had to keep telling myself that.

And when he didn't reply, I wiped away the annoying tears and welcomed anger in. Anger at myself for replying so quickly to him when I saw his text. I should have left it alone.

Sighing, I put the phone away and went to grab my lunch off the floor. Taking it to the bed, I sat down to eat, but I wasn't feeling hungry all of a sudden. Instead, I placed it on the floor and curled my knees up to my chest. I'd allow the memory of his voice to float through my mind. It would help to keep me going until I could be free, either living or not.

Hours later, and finally done with more tears, I got up from the bed only to sink back down. My legs were weak. I then ate what I could from the plate. Half of the peanut butter sandwich. I used to eat twice as much, but I couldn't stomach it any longer. I knew the weight I'd lost could be a danger in the end. If I got sick, I couldn't be sure I'd bounce back from it.

It could be a blessing. But when I still felt there was a chance, it was simply another nightmare I had to face. At least I had a substantial amount of water from the sink in the small bathroom, so I knew I would never dehydrate. If I remembered correctly, a person could live on little to no food for a long time if all they had was water.

I just had to pray any type of sickness, where I couldn't make my way across the room to that water, wouldn't come to fruition.

What would be better was if Gloria or Lenny got sick enough to die. But I wasn't sure Harriet would be safe even then. Gloria could still call the other men to deal with Harriet and her family.

But that was if either Gloria or Lenny called them.

If they didn't call, I could get help, and Harriet would be fine.

Why hadn't I thought of it before?

Maybe because stupid fear had kept me crippled for so long.

I'd seen two people die. I didn't want any more deaths to happen.

My mind tripped over random thoughts. Thoughts I shouldn't have been thinking because they were connected to more death.

Of Gloria and Lenny.

Groaning, I rubbed a hand over my face. It was impossible. I didn't have the strength to go against Gloria or Lenny. I couldn't see anything happening to them. Not enough to see their lives ended where they wouldn't contact their people. I certainly couldn't kill them, nor did I know anyone who could. Risking more people would be foolish. I thought to ring the police, get them to Harriet's before they came here, but then Gloria still had time to call the others. And even with the police at Harriet's, the others could somehow slip by and kill them, while killing the police in the process.

At every turn, all I saw was more death.

Once again, I was out of luck with my new thoughts, so I pushed them aside.

Harriet would stay safe, and I'd go back to waiting until my visit to the attorney for a chance at escape.

God, I would give anything to go back to the days where horse shit, morning and afternoon chores, and homework were the only things I worried about.

Instead, it was all dark, dooming thoughts plaguing my mind.

That was until the previous night when I'd heard beauty.

Shit, Emerson. Stop thinking about him.

It was hard though, because I'd gone without contact for so long. Yet there was now a man asking and willing to help without even knowing me.

Damn him for moving in next door.

For giving my mind *and* body thoughts and reactions I hadn't had in a long time.

Life seriously wasn't fair.

Grimacing, I pushed the plate on the bed and covered it with a blanket to try and stop the bread from drying out. My legs were a little steadier when I climbed to my feet. I needed to make sure I moved around a lot more and not let myself laze about, losing my remaining strength.

I made my way towards the bathroom to wash my hair. I hoped the task would keep my mind off things, even if for only a moment.

I didn't bother removing my clothes. It was time to change them and attempt to clean them after my hair. It didn't matter if they got wet in the process.

The usual thought crossed my mind as I stood before the small sink. I wished I had some shampoo or conditioner; even soap would have been good. However, water would do. Like it always had.

Turning on the water, I picked up the small plastic cup I'd found lying around. I filled it, leaned over the sink, and poured it over my hair, cringing from the coldness. Still, I kept at it, and it wasn't until I was done that I realised I'd been humming to the song Ryan had sung for me.

A pang of sadness swept through me. I wanted to run to my phone to see if he had replied in the end, but I had to stay strong. Even if he had, it wouldn't change my mind.

As I dried my hair with an old T-shirt, I glanced out the window to see the day was overcast. However, the basement remained warm no matter the weather outside, which I was grateful for in the winter months. I went over to a box and picked out fresh—to some extent—clothes. A man's old T-shirt with some logo I'd never seen before on the front. It came down to my knees, like most of the clothes I'd salvaged from the boxes. I could wear it as a dress, but I would never want to walk around in just my underwear alone underneath. Digging deeper in the box, I pulled out a pair of cut-off leggings I'd worn only a couple of times before. Previously they had been too tight for me. Now they sat comfortably around my waist.

My body used to be in good shape, especially from working on the farm. But after years of nothing, my collarbones were visible and my ribs stood out. While I had pretty much two solid meals a day, the calories didn't seem to do their part. I didn't understand how I'd gotten so thin.

In the clear space in front of the bed, I placed a blanket and laid it out flat. Standing on it, I sank to the floor, lying down.

I pulled my body up. Well, tried to. I got halfway—grunting and panting—before dropping back. I'd been slack on my exercises, having felt weakened, but I had to do them.

I dropped an arm over my face, only to feel the hard ridges of my scars. I pulled my arm back enough to stare at the raised lines. I ran my fingers over them. More scars lined my thighs, stopping just above my knees. I trailed my fingers to my chest and felt the ones there.

There were fewer than on my arms and thighs, but enough to be noticeable.

I let my arms fall to the floor and stared up at the roof.

Footsteps banged from above, meaning someone had just come home or gotten out of bed or stood from the couch to go into the kitchen. Since the kitchen was right above where I was, the footsteps sounded louder, so I knew it was their destination.

Lifting a hand, I stuck my middle finger up at the roof.

Fuck them.

Fuck what they do.

Fuck how they are.

Fucking fuck them.

A laugh escaped me, but it cut off into a sob.

Fuck me.

Fuck my life.

Was my hope worth having?

If I didn't have Harriet to think of, I would walk up those stairs, bang on the door, and punch whoever answered it in the face. Then they might kill me.

Then again, I didn't have it in me to do it.

I was weak, not only in body but in mind.

The one good thing I had, I'd pushed away. It had to be done though. At least I could give a person something in my miserable existence.

Safety. As long as I did what I was told... and I would for them.

CHAPTER NINE

WARDEN

*I*t'd been nearly fucking two weeks without a word from Emmie. I didn't know if I should worry or what. Knew she'd said she wouldn't text anymore, but what was the reason for it? I'd sent text after text without an answer to any of my random questions. In the last couple of days, I'd even begged for her to tell me she was all right. Shit, I'd called once or twice as well, but the phone had been switched off, and since her number came from one of those fucking apps that the police and private investigators hated because it wasn't traceable, I was shit out of luck finding the location of it.

She wasn't the only thing putting me in a goddamn foul mood. Shanti had been a dead end. All of the other night-time employees had been a dead end too. Though, they all said the same thing: ask the manager when he got back.

I swore to Christ, if this guy didn't have anything for me, there'd be hell. I wanted answers to give the mother. I wanted the people responsible for destroying her daughter's life to pay.

I wanted fucking blood.

What I didn't want was to be told to have the afternoon off.

But the others at work were caught up on their own cases, and since I was at a standstill until fuckhead got back, Violet ordered us to get some much-needed rest. The woman didn't leave the office until she knew I was out the door because she wasn't dumb; I would have stayed and tried to find another clue to my case.

On the way home, my thoughts returned to Emmie. Then I was pissed all over again, as even my late-night singing didn't have her reaching out either.

Slamming through my back door, I stood on my deck in the afternoon sun. I pulled my sunglasses down over my eyes and glared out at the houses around me.

Emmie was in one of those. She had to have been to have heard my music.

"Emmie," I called. Nothing. Fuck, she was probably at work, but I doubted it because I still thought that was a lie.

Dragging my phone out of my back pocket, I called out again, my tone rougher from annoyance, "Emmie." Out the corner of my eye, I thought I saw movement down near the ground. But when I looked, there was nothing but a window to the neighbour's basement. I didn't know the people. I had their names when I looked into the folks around the area, but that was it. "Emmie," I barked louder.

Nothing.

Sighing, I ran a hand through my hair. "Emmie, answer your damn phone," I clipped, louder still.

My phone beeped. I opened it.

Emmie: Shut up.

There was a follow-up beep.

Emmie: Please, shut up. Please.

Worry twisted my gut. She was in trouble.

Ryan: Are you okay?

"Hey, man" was called. I turned to the side, seeing a guy in his late twenties maybe. He looked like he'd been on a bender all night and could use a shower.

"Hey," I replied.

His eyes twitched. "Heard you calling someone. All good?" He sniffed, ran a hand over his face, and I caught his quick look down at the window by his feet.

"Yeah, ah…"

"Lenny," he supplied.

Lenny Kavas and Gloria Summers. I recalled their names from the information I got. Obviously not married, but together or just roommates.

"Right, Lenny." I waved my phone in my hand. "Was tryin' to get my woman to answer her phone. Left some messages."

He huffed. "Woman troubles. Never ends, right, brother?"

I nearly screwed my face up at him. He didn't have the fucking right to call me brother. First impression of the guy already had me on edge. There was something about him I didn't like. Besides, he looked like a druggie and didn't really introduce himself as my neighbour, just wanted to see what I was doing yelling out.

"That's right."

"What's her name?"

Why in the fuck would he want to know that?

"Emily," I said. "Cute name, but she can be a stubborn pain in my arse."

Lenny chuckled. "Can't they all."

"You talk like you got one. By the way, name's Jackson. Moved in here nearly two months ago."

"Yeah." He nodded. "Heard. And, ah, like I said, name's Lenny, and my missus is Gloria."

"Just you two living there?"

His eye twitched. "Sure is."

With my eyes covered by sunglasses, I glanced down at the

window and I was sure to fucking Christ I saw fingers there for a second before disappearing.

"Your lady at home? Maybe I could meet her. She might know some other birds around here since it seems I won't have this one for much longer."

Lenny laughed. "Nah, brother, she ain't home right now."

Big blaring alarm bells rang through my head. I did see something; there were fingers in the tiny goddamn window. So whose were they?

"Too bad. Maybe another time."

"Yeah. Sounds good." He kicked at the ground. I started to turn when he questioned, "You work around here?"

"Just outta town. Mining."

"Right, cool." He nodded. "Guess I'll see you around."

I put out a fake, friendly smile. "Maybe, maybe not. The hours are crazy."

He laughed. "Yeah, I heard that. I couldn't do it."

"You work?"

"Not right now."

"Always a place at mining. We go through a lot of people."

"Not for me, brother." He grinned, sent a salute, and walked off to the front of his house.

It wasn't until he was out of sight that a message came through.

Emmie: Please don't call my name.

Ryan: Tell me you're safe.

Emmie: I'm safe.

Ryan: Tell me it's not you in that fucking basement.

Pressure shot to my chest when no reply came.

Ryan: I can get you out.

Emmie: No!

I clenched my jaw.

Ryan: Why the fuck not?

Emmie: I just can't. Not yet.

I heard the rev of an engine flying up the road. It came to a screeching halt out the front of the neighbour's house.

Emmie: Go inside. Don't worry about me.

Ryan: Emmie. I can't do that.

A woman climbed out of the car and headed for the front door at a swift pace.

Emmie: Please, please go inside. I have to hide my phone. Don't text. PLEASE.

Fuck.

Motherfucking hell. It felt wrong. I wanted to storm the place, but I didn't. Instead, with a burning gut, I spun and stalked back inside. I paced just inside the closed door, phone gripped in hand. I wanted to text, to call, but her plea kept rolling in my mind. I had to fucking wait until I knew that fucker Lenny and his woman were either out or asleep.

I was never good at waiting.

Pressing a name in my contacts, I lifted my phone to my ear. Violet answered after the third ring with a laugh. "I told you to have the damn afternoon off."

"You need to come here."

"What's going on?" Any trace of humour she'd held in her voice vanished.

"I don't know."

"I'm on my way. Do you need me to call in Butch?"

"I'll do it." It'd give me something to do.

"Right. See you soon," she said, then hung up.

I pressed Butch's name. He answered with "Hey, I was just about to call you. My guy at the airport in Melbourne rang. That manager, Jarrod Daltron, just landed. Got home early it seems. It'll take him at least an hour and a half to get back here. You want me to come with you when you question him?"

"You're gonna have to do it. I've got something goin' on."

"You good?"

I blew out a breath. "I don't fuckin' know what to think of it. Got Vi coming over. You head here after you see that guy. I'll send through what I have on the case for you to have a quick look over."

"Right. On it."

"Thanks."

"Sure you don't need me earlier? The manager can wait until tomorrow."

"No. Get that done for me. Then come here."

"Will do. Later," he said, then disconnected without a reply from me.

It'd take Vi at least half an hour to get to my place since she lived out of town in her soon-to-be husband's house. Fuck, what was I gonna do with my time?

One thing I could do…. I pressed another name on the phone. A new connection the firm had, who came to us when Mally had her shit go down. We had others in the police force, but no one like Lan Davis. He did things differently than the others. He'd had the Hawks MC's backs behind the line of duty.

"Lan Davis."

"Lan. Warden here. I work with—"

"Ryan Warden, works for Violet Marcus, Talon's sister. Know who you are. What can I do for you?"

"I'm not sure yet. This is what I do know." I told him everything I could about Emmie. He listened silently. "What do you think?" I asked at the end.

"I think you can't do anything without proof, and some texts won't do without a photo. What makes things hard is how this woman isn't willin' for help. What's stopping her? There's more we need to find out, but for now, I'll get what I can on Lenny and Gloria. Give you a call when I have it."

Relief was instant. Some of the tightness in my chest lessened. Fucking hell, I'd made the right choice by bringing him in. Yeah, we could do our own background work, but I was sure Lan could do it faster. Besides, I wanted to stay close and keep an eye on the place next door.

"Appreciate it, Lan."

"Anytime," he said before hanging up.

I moved to the back door again and peered out. I couldn't see the window to the basement; it was just out of sight. I opened the back door but left the screen closed. I strained to hear anything, but not a sound reached my ears.

I goddamn hated not knowing what was going on.

What did Emmie have to deal with?

Who was she?

Why was she in the basement?

Who in the fuck was Gloria or Lenny to her?

Why didn't Emmie want to leave?

So many fucking questions, and I was determined to get the answers.

CHAPTER TEN

EMERSON

A FEW MOMENTS EARLIER

As I sat on the bed, I held the phone in my hand and stared down at all the messages Ryan had sent. Not only were there messages, but he'd tried calling a couple of times. I didn't know why, but that day my resolve had diminished, and I'd taken out the phone to see if he had contacted me. I'd been strong, like I promised myself, except for then.

Maybe it was because I was missing my dad more that day since it was his birthday and I wanted some type of contact with the real world, even for just a moment.

I hadn't expected to find all the messages.

He'd started out telling me how he didn't care if I didn't message back, he just wanted to reach out.

Then it continued from there.

Favourite food? Mine's nachos.

Do you read? I don't. I've tried but I fall asleep too fast.

Do you like sports? I do. Football.

Is Emmie short for something? Emily?

Emmanuel?

Emma?

My smile had grown with each suggestion. With each message. Not all of these texts were on the same day either.

Emmit?

Screw that, sounds like a guy's name.

Emmalise?

Forget it, I've probably guessed it right already or your name is just Emmie.

I'm about to smack the shit outta Butch, a guy I work with. He ate my damn lunch again.

Are you okay?

I feel like a fucking idiot messaging when I'm not getting a reply, but I'm gonna still do it.

Do you like Disney? A friend of mine does but I don't see the point in watching it.

Some days I hate my job when I can't find the answers I want.

He wasn't just asking me things; he was also giving. Reading all of his responses was yet another something special he was giving me. I knew he liked to run, drink beer over spirits, read the comics in the newspaper, sing. But he also told me he'd never sung in front of anyone before. I was the first. He didn't like the attention. No matter what Butch said about him being a ladies' man and sucking up all the attention for himself when they went out, it was—in his words—bullshit. He was a loner when he could be, but it seemed his friends list was growing each year, and he was glad for it.

My eyes widened when I heard "Emmie" called loudly.

"No, no, no," I chanted, climbing on top of the bed to peer out the window. When I saw Ryan standing on the back deck, I slammed my back into the wall out of sight. Only I still gripped the window edge to keep from falling.

"Emmie" was clipped roughly. I wavered on my feet. Why was he calling me? My hand left the window edge to grip at my chest. I needed to reach inside myself and hold my heart to steady the fast beating. When I heard footsteps above me, fear rolled my stomach. If they heard him, they could put two and two together. If they even guessed he was calling out for me, I didn't know what would happen. All I could see was more blood and death flashing through my mind.

"Emmie" was snapped, louder than before.

I heard the front door open. With trembling hands, I quickly texted, **Shut up**. Only I didn't think it was enough, so I sent another: **Please, shut up. Please.**

Then my throat closed over when I heard, "Hey, man." Lenny was out there talking to Ryan.

Please, please don't say anything about me. When Ryan replied with a greeting, Lenny went right into questioning him. After Ryan said he was calling his girl named Emily, some tension eased from my shoulders. I chanced a glance out the window. Lenny stood right near it, so I quickly moved away. What I couldn't understand was why Ryan gave Lenny a different name.

Confusion drew my brows together, my pulse raced, and as soon as I heard Lenny leave, I quickly shot off a text to Ryan, telling him not to call my name again. If Gloria got home and Lenny told her anything about what Ryan said, I knew she would come down questioning me.

Tears threatened, but I closed my eyes tightly to blink them away. My phone vibrated. Ryan asked me if I was safe. I was for now, but I only told him I was.

His next message had me gasping. **Tell me it's not you in that fucking basement.**

I didn't know what to say. How had he known? Did he see me? It was hard to say since I didn't see him once look that way, but he also had sunglasses on that didn't show his eyes.

When I didn't reply, he sent another. **I can get you out.**

Panic seized me. **No!** I quickly replied.

Ryan: Why the fuck not?

He wouldn't understand. He didn't know, and all I wanted to do was hide the phone. My fingers flew over the letters. **I just can't. Not yet.**

My ears pricked up at the sound of an engine revving hard out the front.

Gloria was home.

I gripped my phone. **Go inside. Don't worry about me.** I tried.

Ryan: Emmie. I can't do that.

Gloria must have slammed her door hard enough for it to ring through the neighbourhood. She couldn't catch me with my phone.

Emmie: Please, please go inside. I have to hide my phone. Don't text. PLEASE, I begged, before running across the room and slipping the phone away. I didn't know if Ryan would do as I asked, but I hoped. I really hoped.

Voices above rose. I quickly raced back to the bed and sat on it, curling my legs up to wrap my arms around my knees.

What would Lenny tell Gloria?

Was he suspicious at all?

Why did he go outside when Ryan was calling out?

Did I screw everything up?

My heart hammered hard in my chest. I didn't know what to think, what to do; all I could do was wait. Why did I message a man who seemed to care?

I should have left it alone.

Why had Ryan lied about his name?

If Ryan saw me, did that mean Lenny also did?

Footsteps pounded on the floor above. I gripped my arms tightly, knowing I would probably bruise from it, but I couldn't stop.

The door opened, someone slammed their feet on the stairs.

Gloria's jean-clad legs came into view.

Shit, shit, shit.

Did she have a weapon on her? Would she consider killing Ryan? Was Lenny smart enough to actually suspect something?

Her hard gaze clashed with mine.

Jesus, what would I usually do when she came down? Did my expression give anything away? Was I actually looking normal?

"Did you speak with the neighbour?" she asked, crossing her arms over her chest.

"What? No." I shook my head.

Her lips thinned. She stormed forward. I raised my arms, batted at her hands, but she managed to grab my hair and neck, tugging me roughly from the bed. She shook me. I gripped at each of her wrists to try and stop the lack of air and scalding pain shooting over my scalp.

"Did you talk to the neighbour?" she demanded, spittle dripping from her mouth.

"No!" I choked.

She dropped her hold. When my body slumped to the floor, I dragged in ragged breaths. How could I make her believe me? I didn't see an option. I would just try as I was and hope I wasn't too hurt by the end of it.

"I'll ask one more time. Did you talk to the neighbour?"

I shook my head.

"Answer me," she snarled before her booted foot connected to my stomach.

"No!" I yelled, folding in on myself. "No, no, no," I repeated again and again.

My hair was gripped once more, my head forced back so she could stare down at my tear-streaked face. "If I find out you have, I'm heading over to that bitch's place and will make sure she pays for your lies."

"I didn't. I haven't said anything. W-why are you asking me?"

Please, please believe me.

"Gloria," Lenny called down the stairs. "A car just pulled up next door."

"Better start praying nothing comes to bite us on the arse," she threatened before throwing her hand out, still attached to my hair. I fell to my back from the force. She swiftly left the room.

Slowly, I sat up, wincing from the ache in my stomach. At least this time I didn't think anything was broken. A door above opened and closed with force. Sounds of muffled voices touched my ears. Standing, I staggered over to the bed and climbed on. I moved my head to the side so my ear was closer to the opened window. Only it didn't help to clear the voices up. They must have been all the way out the front.

Sighing, I shifted around and slid down to sit on the bed. I cringed. My hands went to my stomach to rest against it. A new bruise would appear later, or at least by the next day.

Still, it was worth it. Keeping Ryan safe would always be worth it.

I crossed my fingers and prayed Gloria didn't come back in, knowing somehow I had lied.

If she did, I wasn't sure she'd keep me around for me to inherit the money. Then again, I wasn't sure Ryan would sit by and let me stay in here with them... but he had to. I had to make him see sense, that saving lives over mine was more important to me than anything.

Could I tell him everything?

Would he understand?

Harriet's and her family's lives were at stake, so he had to understand.

He had to.

Not only for Harriet, but for his life, his friends'. If Gloria found out anything, they would all be hunted. Unless Ryan got to her first....

Groaning, I hit my head against the wall behind me.

There I went again, giving myself hope that I could escape this hellhole sooner than I would be able to when I tried on my own.

It was because I believed Ryan, how he'd said he couldn't leave me where I was. He seemed like a man who would do anything for someone in need, or was I just playing him up in my mind? Matching him to the stars I already had in my eyes for him?

My body jolted when a door above slammed. I waited for the dooming footsteps to come my way. When they didn't, I sighed in relief. Whatever Ryan had said or whoever turned up at his place had somehow shown Gloria I wasn't at fault.

How long would that last though?

CHAPTER ELEVEN

WARDEN

*M*y phone stayed silent. Even when I pressed the button to light up the screen over and over, nothing new appeared. My gut felt shredded from the worry. I'd thought I'd heard someone yell not a few moments before, and I wanted to run over there, barge through the door, and demand to know what in the ever-loving fuck was going on.

But I didn't.

I hated that I didn't. I hated that Emmie begged for me not to call her name and to stop messaging, but I did it. For her. A woman I didn't know. All because I was concerned for her.

I pressed in Violet's number. "Talk," she answered.

"You nearly here?"

"Yes."

"Travis with you?"

"When a partner calls, says to get to his place and you're not sure why, you think he'll come with?"

He would. For his woman.

"You'll have to pull over a block away. Tell Travis to make his way to the backyard on foot."

She sucked in a breath. "What the fuck, Warden?"

"Look, somethin's happenin' next door. Need you to show on your own. Your name's Emily. Mine's Jackson, and you're my girl, but we've had a fight."

She gave me nothing but silence.

"Vi, whatever is goin' on next door is bad. I got a read off the guy Lenny, and I didn't fuckin' like it at all. What I do know is that there's a woman locked in a basement. At least, I think she is. I told her I could help, but she doesn't want it."

"We're nearing. I'll get Travis to come through on foot. He's heard you and said if you try and make a move on me, he'll rip your balls off."

I snorted. He could try, but I had about ten pounds on the guy. I'd put up a big fight. Not that I wanted to make a move on Vi. Christ, she was like a sister.

"I'll be sure to keep it clean. This is a just in case. Not even sure they'll be watchin'."

"Be there shortly," she said, then hung up.

Sighing, I tapped my phone to my forehead before pocketing it and making my way to the front of the house. True to her word, Vi was there shortly. Her car came to a screeching stop out the front of my place. She got out and glared up at my house. I went to the door and opened it.

"What you doin' here, woman?" I called loudly.

"Call me woman again and I'll leave," Vi answered.

We both kept our eyes on each other even when we heard the door bang open next door. It was soon closed with a slam.

"Since I left voice messages not that long ago without an answer back, I thought you weren't talkin' to me, dumplin'."

Vi's eyes narrowed even more. They told me I'd pay for the dumplin'. "You sounded like a sorry arse on the phone. Guess I needed to see it in person."

"Come inside, Emily," I said, crossing my arms over my chest.

"You ready to grovel, Jackson?"

We heard a sound, like someone grunted after being hit. "Hey, man," Lenny called, and from the way he was rubbing his rib standing on their front porch next to his woman, I knew he'd taken an elbow to the side. She wanted him to get our attention.

Well, it happened, and I wanted to see what they'd say.

"Hey," I called back.

"This is my woman, Gloria."

"Hi." She smiled, but it didn't reach her hard eyes.

I gave her a chin lift, and when Violet got to my side, I curled an arm around her shoulders. "This is Emily."

Violet waved. "Hi. Nice to meet someone around here."

"Haven't really seen you here before," Gloria commented.

"That's because I have a better place than Jackson's."

When I caught Lenny's look of "is she serious," I nodded.

"If she wasn't good at givin' head, she'd be long gone." For that, I got a fist to the gut. I coughed and started laughing. I grabbed her wrist before she tried it again. "Come on, dingleberry, you know I'm messin'."

Lenny let out a snort. "Dingleberry?"

I squished Vi to my side. "My woman loves the pet names. The more unique, the better." Leaning towards them, I added on a pretend whisper, "But I only use Emmie when I know I'm in the doghouse."

Christ, it was making me sick acting this shit out.

I knew Vi would be feeling it too. What also gave it away was when her hand landed on my waist and she pinched me fucking hard. "How about we go in before you tell them all our damn secrets. Nice to meet you both."

"Yeah, same," Gloria said.

"Enjoy, brother," Lenny said. Damn, the guy was stupid. I wasn't completely sure we'd sold Gloria on our story, but I hoped Lenny's stupidity would rub off on her.

I sent him a salute with a smirk that hopefully fucking said I was about to get me some.

Once inside the front door, I spotted Travis sitting on the couch. Before I could say anything, Vi dropped her arm, turned to me, and yelled, "Now tell me why I should forgive you for making out with my brother, Jackson. My brother!"

Grinding my teeth together, I mouthed, "You fuckin' bitch."

"Emmie, sweetheart, I told you already I didn't know it was him. It was dark. I thought it was you climbing into bed, not him."

Travis snorted softly.

Her lips thinned to stop from laughing. "I don't know if I can believe you."

"Come here, let me make it up to you." I lifted a finger to my lips and jerked my head towards the stairs. I started for them, and Violet let out a loud moan before she tipped my damn lamp off the side table. It crashed to the floor and she cried out, "Yes, He-Man, yes."

For fuck's sake. Guess at least she was selling me as being good in the sack.

Shaking my head, I walked up the stairs knowing they'd both follow me. I took them into the study on the far side of the house, away from next door. When we were all in, I shut the door. Violet went to my desk and sat behind it. Travis parked his arse on the edge near her. Great, I was going to have to disinfect the hell out of it.

"A couple of weeks ago, I got a text late one night from an unknown number. She wouldn't tell me how she got it but that she just wanted to reach out. The name she gave me was Emmie." There was no fucking way I'd tell them it was because my singing "soothed" her. "I looked into the people around my house and came up empty-handed. I tried to find out more, but she backed off. It was somethin' in her text that had me concerned for her. I couldn't pin it down, until just before I called you." I paced, running a hand through my hair. "When she stopped communicating, I kept messagin' her random shit to see if she'd open up. She didn't. Not a single message back. But that changed when earlier, I went out on my back deck and started calling her name. She frantically texted me tellin' me to be quiet. That was when Lenny, the dickhead next door, came out. Thought it was strange he'd appear after me being here for nearly two months. He questioned who I was yellin' out to. I got a read on him that something was up. I asked if he was alone. He said his woman was out. I acted as if my pretend girl, Emily, was gonna give me shit, said I'd be lookin' for something else, that maybe his woman would know someone. Thing was, when he'd said his woman was out, I caught movement in their basement window."

"Fuck," Travis clipped.

"Who is she?"

"Don't have a fuckin' clue. She won't tell me anything. She's scared. I know that much. They've got something over her or are threatenin' her with something."

"You want her out?" Vi queried.

"Fuck yes, but I need to make sure she'll be safe when it happens. Need to know what they've got that's keepin' her wanting to be locked up."

"You know for certain she's locked up?" Violet asked.

"Never seen anyone around that house except for those two fuckers. I got a good indication she's trapped down there."

"How do you want to lead this?"

"Got Lan looking into them. See what he can find out. Spoke to Butch. He's on my other case following the lead. For now, we need to watch the house, and I'm gonna try and talk to her some more through text."

"Do you have any more information from Emmie?"

"She says she's safe. Gotta believe it for now. Says she's thirty, but not sure if I can believe that. I told her I could get her out. She said no. Not yet."

"Which is why you think they have something over her," Travis commented.

I nodded. "We need to set up cameras, front and back. I have some equipment here, but I'll need more."

"I'll make a trip to work, grab what you need. Make a list."

I went to my desk and grabbed a pen and paper, jotting down what I'd need.

"If you don't have everything at work, I'll get Link on to finding it," Travis said. Link was his man. Heard of the guy, just hadn't met him. I grunted in response.

My phone vibrated. Dropping the pen, I took it out and my chest tightened.

"It's her," I bit out.

"What did she say?" Violet asked.

"Please know I appreciate your offer for help, but I can't accept it. I won't have anyone else hurt because of me. You need to stay away from Lenny and Gloria. Stay safe, Warden. One day I will get out of here, away from them. But until then, I can't communicate anymore. I promise I'll be free one day. One way or another. You've helped me by talking to me. I'll always treasure the small gift you've given me, but please, please, Warden, stay away and be safe. I won't let them darken your door again. If you just go on with your days as you were and pretend I don't exist, it would be better for all of us. Thank you, and I'm sorry." I gripped the phone. If I didn't need it, I would have fucking crushed the damn thing or thrown it.

"She doesn't want anyone else hurt because of her," Violet

said. "Who have they hurt?"

I shook my head, not having a goddamn answer.

"She's protecting you from them," Travis said.

"She is," I said, my tone rough. She didn't know me, know what I was capable of, and yet she wanted to protect me because she feared I'd be hurt by those fuckers. I could get her out. I *had* to get her out.

"Are you going to reply?" Violet asked.

I wanted to. Wanted to tell her she was crazy if she thought I'd listen and wouldn't do anything, but that'd just make her worry. I didn't want that.

"I'll leave it," I told them.

"For now," Travis added.

"Yeah, for fuckin' now."

"What do you think she meant by being free one day and in one way or another?"

That part I didn't like. It left my gut coiled in worry.

No one said anything for a moment.

Until Travis did. "We're all thinking the same thing. She's either going to run somehow or die trying to get free."

"It won't happen," I snarled.

Violet stood and came to my side, placing her hand on my arm. "No, it won't. I'll go get the things you need."

"Sweetheart," Travis called. "If you leave now, it'll look suspicious. As far as they know, you two have"—his upper lip rose—"fucked. I'll go out and get the items. I'll catch a cab when I'm far enough away. I'll just need the keys."

"Shit, you're right." Violet nodded, handing her keys over. Travis gave her a quick kiss to the temple and left. I knew he'd get out and away without being seen. He had skills.

"I hate waiting," Violet said, heading back to the chair.

She wasn't the only one. If I didn't get some type of answer to any of my questions soon, I'd fucking lose it.

CHAPTER TWELVE

WARDEN

*I*t'd been about an hour, and I was back to pacing the damn floor in the tiny fucking room. Travis should be back soon and then at least I'd have something to do while setting up the system. I rocked my head side to side to try and lessen the tension in my neck, but it wouldn't let up. I'd been up and down the stairs a million times to see if I could see or hear anything from next door, but it was quiet.

When there was a knock on my front door, Violet looked up from the computer and met my gaze. "I don't know," I told her curious eyes. We both made our way out of the room, down the stairs, and to the front door.

"Wait," Violet whispered before I could open it. She undid a couple of buttons on her shirt, ruffled her hair. "In case it's them, we need to look like we did it."

Christ, she was right. I quickly pulled off my tee and threw it towards the couch. She nodded. I grabbed the handle, thinking I had to fucking invest in a peephole, and opened the door.

Butch's eyes came to me from the open doorway when I

swung the door open. He opened his mouth to talk but snapped it closed. He looked at me, over my shoulder, to me, then back over my shoulder. When his eyes shot back to me, he asked, "You got a death wish? Does Travis know about this?"

Rolling my eyes, I ordered, "Just get the fuck in here."

Shaking his head, he stepped in. When he was clear of the front door, I closed it.

"What is this?" Butch asked, gesturing with his hand to Violet and then me.

"You seriously think I would go there?" I demanded.

"Hey." Violet glared.

"Well, no, but… the clothes say otherwise."

Sighing, I pinched the bridge of my nose. Then I explained to Butch what was going on. By the end of it, we were sitting in the kitchen with a beer. I'd deemed it safe for us to wander the house since if they saw Butch arrive or his car out front, they'd know we wouldn't be in bed.

"Sounds messed up. Want to know something strange though?" He didn't wait for an answer, just continued, "The manager guy from the club I went to see seemed tweaked by my visit and questions. Well, his car is next door right now."

My beer hit the table as I leaned towards him. "What the fuck?"

Butch nodded. "He must have just got here before I did, but I'd pulled up to grab a snack on the way."

I glanced at Violet. "They're in on it?"

She shrugged. "Could be. Highly likely."

I looked back to Butch. "You think this guy deals the drugs to the girls?"

"Man, I can't say for certain, but the dude was suspicious. He wouldn't meet my gaze the whole time. Kept saying how tired he was after getting back. Now he's next door, and with what you've told me about the characters there, it's starting to connect some serious dots in my head."

"Same here." I nodded. If that was the case, I wanted to put pressure on the three of them about the drugged-out girls and why the hell Emmie was kept in the basement. Question was, did I go about it the legal way or another? Right then, all I could see was the other way because I had the biggest fucking feeling Emmie needed to get out of there. How long had she been in there in the first place?

"What are you thinking?" Violet asked.

"Do we go in now, hard and fast, *make* them tell us everything they know, and help the woman in their basement? Or play it safe and have all the evidence we need to convict them?"

"What happens if we do it fast and it backfires? Remember what Emmie said; she won't let anyone else get hurt because of her. Do they have someone she's trying to save, which is why she's staying there?"

Fuck. If there was, it could mean risking that person if they were at another destination.

"I need her to tell me."

Violet nodded. "You do."

I snatched up my phone from the table and typed out a text. "How's this sound? 'Emmie, before I can let this drop, like you asked, I need more information first.'"

"It's a good start. She won't know what your questions will be, but she'll be willing to answer them to protect you." Violet said. I pressed Send and we all stared down at the phone.

I ground my teeth together when no text came back right away.

Movement in the laundry room caught my attention. I looked there to see Travis stepping through the side door, his arm curled around a box. Violet stood, walking over to him.

He stopped, their heads bent together. She was telling him what we'd learned from Butch.

After a few moments, they came into the kitchen with Violet saying, "For now, we're just waiting on a text from Emmie."

"If we fuckin' get one," I added.

"She will," Violet said, sounding sure.

Yeah, I had a feeling Emmie would text back, but I was an impatient man. I wanted it now, and I had a feeling it wouldn't be.

"Violet said you're thinking of going in for the three of them," Travis said, taking a seat next to his woman.

"Just an option to think about," I told him.

"What happens if there's more people in their group? We don't know if it's only drugging girls and dumping them that they're doing. We don't know how many are involved. Are you willing to let the crew next door be taken in and then they contact their people? We don't know how dangerous they are. They could come for this Emmie woman or the people she's worried about."

Jesus motherfucking Christ. He was right.

Going in with force was out of the damn question until we had more answers.

"They could tell us who they work with," Butch said.

"Or they couldn't. Not many men"—he glanced at Violet —"or women would rat out their partners."

"It's a risk we can't take right now. Not until we know more."

"Agreed." Violet nodded.

My phone rang. I quickly looked to the caller ID. Disappointment swept through me when it wasn't a blocked number. Instead, it was Lan. "Lan," I answered.

"Lenny Kavas and Gloria Summers have been living in that

house for five years. From what I can tell, they've never had a job, been on the dole since then. Two years ago or just over, Gloria's niece came to live with them." My body locked tight. "She attended a local school until a friend of the family paid for her to attend a boarding school in Melbourne."

"What's her name?" I clipped through clenched teeth.

"Emerson Spence."

Emerson.

Emmie.

"You know what I'm thinkin'?" I asked Lan.

"That Emerson isn't really at a school, but in the basement next door to you. They've got some decoy at the school instead."

"Yes," I hissed.

"A friend owes me a favour. She's on her way to the boarding school now. I'll see what she can find out. What I don't understand is why bring in a stranger to pretend to be Emerson in the first place?"

"That's something we need to find out. Look, we've learnt more too." I told him what Butch told me, even while my gut ate at my organs.

Emerson Spence was a teenager.

A fucking teen.

She'd told me she was thirty. Why?

"I'm not liking this at all, Warden. I think the station—"

"I'm on this."

"But—"

"I'm on this, Lan. I appreciate the help like I said, but this is our case."

He sighed. "I get it. I don't like it, but I get it. Look, I'll also look into this family friend who's paid the bill for the boarding school."

"That'd be good," I said.

87

"Talk soon."

"Got it." As soon as I ended the call, I relayed what Lan said to the others. "I'm gonna go set up the cameras." I grabbed the box off the table and started from the room.

"Warden," Violet called. When I faced her, she asked, "Are you all right?"

Was I? No. For some fucking reason, I felt played by Emmie, and yet I didn't have the right to feel that way. So what if she told me she was older than what she was. *She's still a woman in need of help.* That was all I had to remember. I'd do my job, get her out, get her safe and living free. That was all.

"Fine," I bit out.

"Warden," Vi pressed in a tone of warning.

Unclenching my jaw, I said, "Just want this done. Emerson has been in that basement for God knows how long."

Butch stood. "How about I give you a hand with the camera set-up?"

I narrowed my eyes. "You know I don't need it."

He shrugged. "I know, but I hate sitting around doing nothing."

"Let him help," Violet suggested. Damn it all, she was probably worried where my head was. I didn't even know myself. What I did know was that no one deserved to be stuck in a motherfucking basement. Rage ignited in my chest. My hands near crushed the box with the equipment in it. I said nothing more and stalked out of the room and up the stairs to grab the rest of the shit I needed.

It was when we were coming back down the stairs that there was a knock on my front door. "Fuck," I muttered. If it was either of them from next door, I'd be likely to drag them in and kick the fucking shit out of them.

"I'll get it," Violet said, walking into the room. At the bottom of the stairs, I stopped—with Butch behind me—out of view of the door. Violet opened it, stepped back, and let in her brother, Talon Marcus, president of the Hawks Motorcycle Club. Following him were his most trusted brothers. Griz, Blue, Killer, and Stoke, who was Mally's man. Shit, they all had good women to call their own.

Talon gave me a chin lift. Then he gestured to Griz and pointed over to my entertainment unit. When the door was shut, I made my way over. "What the fuck is this? If they see the brothers come in here—"

Violet yelled, "Let's get this party started," just before music blared to life. Closing my eyes, I rocked my head side to side, but the tension upped a level with the pounding music.

Opening my eyes, I glared at Violet and pointed towards the kitchen. Before I moved, I caught Talon do some hand movements. Blue and Stoke stayed in the living room, sitting on the couch. Stoke pulled a pack of cards free. He caught me looking and lifted his hand to his mouth, pretending to drink. I wasn't their damn maid.

A hand slapped my shoulder. "I'll grab them a beer," Butch offered. I grunted and went to the kitchen table, setting my things down.

The door between the kitchen and living room closed; the music quieted a bit. Turning, I demanded, "You wanna tell me what the hell is goin' on?"

Violet stepped closer. "I rang them in case we need backup."

"I thought you were down with waiting until we had more information. She hasn't even messaged back."

"That was until I spoke to Talon," she said, then shifted back enough for her brother to step up. Butch got closer to hear what was being said.

"William Haulder, the manager you're interested in, has been on a lot of radars in the last couple of days. Only we didn't have his full name until now. About a month ago, a girl at Maya's school spread a story about a guy she'd heard of who was selling drugs to underage kids at a club. A week later, that same girl went to this club. She was drugged, raped, and dumped."

"We haven't heard about it from the cops. I'm on a—"

Talon's hand shot up. I ground my teeth together and took a deep breath. "The cops know nothin' about this case; she didn't report it." His upper lip rose in a snarl. "Her mother told her not to. No one would believe her. Maya didn't believe the rumour the girl had spread until a week ago when she caught the girl in the school bathroom trying to kill herself. The girl then confided in Maya about everything. So Maya came and told me. Since then, I've been lookin' into it. Violet's told me everything you know, and when Haulder's name came up, I knew it'd be connected. Especially since you're on the case for that girl in the same situation." He stopped. Was he waiting for me to say something? Was this the dramatic pause people talked about?

Fuck that. "Doesn't explain why you're here."

"Got a tip that the main man for the group is making a drop-off tonight. The address happens to be right next door to you."

Fucking hell.

"You're goin' in tonight?"

He nodded once. "As soon as the guy arrives."

"I'm in."

"You all are. But you're gonna be the one walkin' up to the front door."

I smiled. I was goddamn down for that.

CHAPTER THIRTEEN

EMERSON

*L*oud pumping music filled the air. It seemed Ryan had decided to have a party. Confusion rolled through my mind. Why would he? I didn't think he would be the type of man to go on with his life as if the strange situation next door to him hadn't happened. Yet, there he was.

Glancing to the stairs, I wondered for the millionth time in the last couple of hours if I could risk getting my phone and seeing if Ryan had sent more. But fear had me sitting in the one spot, waiting and listening to what I could from upstairs. I knew someone had arrived, heard muffled voices, but couldn't make anything out. I didn't want to move in case somehow me retrieving my phone could lead to Ryan getting hurt.

I was also scared for myself. Deep down, I knew there was a small fire lit inside me. It burned for more. Burned for love and freedom. For a simple and yet happy life. The fear was ever present though; I worried if I made the wrong move, I would lose it all and my fire would be snuffed out.

My stomach rumbled, but I wouldn't be eating. I didn't have anything left over, and I knew—no, I hoped—Gloria wouldn't bring anything down so I didn't have to see her. I still had a feeling she could read me too well, which was why she didn't really believe what I'd said earlier. I was sure the only reason she wasn't down here was because of whatever Ryan had said or done.

The afternoon was turning into a cooler one. I shivered as the breeze swept through the small window down on to me. I needed to get up and grab the old hooded jumper I'd scavenged, but I couldn't get my body to move. My mind was coherent, only my body wasn't responding. It kept me where I was, waiting for something.

After another hour, or what I thought would be an hour, went by, another person arrived upstairs. I wondered if Gloria was having her own type of party. The thought made me sick. If it was anything like the time I'd walked in.... I couldn't go there with those thoughts. I would spiral down.

The chill in the air had grown. I unfolded myself from the bed and went over to the hoodie, quickly pulling it on. I grabbed the socks as well, slipping into them, nearly falling over in the process because dizziness swarmed my head when I bent over. I gripped a box to hold me up. Only the old cardboard folded under my weight; I fell to the ground on my hands and knees.

That was when I heard it. Heavy pounding on the front door above.

I froze there on the cold concrete and listened, wishing my hearing was stronger than it was. Immediately, I threw that wish away when I heard, "Yo, Jackson, what's happening?"

Ryan was there.

Why was Ryan there?

My pulse raced. I could *feel* the beat in my neck.

His voice was too low for me to hear, but then laughter came through.

What was happening?

I needed to know, and yet I didn't want to.

He wouldn't... no, he couldn't tell them he knew about me, right?

I fell back to my bottom, gripping my stomach as it threatened to revolt in fear.

I wouldn't allow myself to believe for a second that Ryan would do that to me. Not when he offered help in the first place.

My eyes widened. I sucked in a ragged breath. He wouldn't be there now to try and help me, would he? Not after my asking him not to.

Suddenly, feet appeared on the bottom stairs. I hadn't heard them. I hadn't heard the door open or close. I let a squeak drop from my lips before I slapped a hand over them. I scooted back on my butt to the corner.

The feet belonged to a man. They were covered in large boots.

Mean boots.

Could boots even be mean?

What was I thinking?

The body came into view. I choked on a noise when I saw a rough-looking man with tattoos all over him.

His eyes swung right to me. His hands came up. One out in front of him, the other lifted a finger went over his lips in a shushing motion. He took a couple of steps towards me, and I scooted behind boxes into a corner.

His hand pressed down into the air in front of him. "Settle," he whispered on a growl. "I'm with Warden."

Warden?

Who was Warden? My mind was too wired with fear that it didn't place.

He must have read the confusion on me because he added, "The guy next door."

Ryan.

Why would Ryan send a guy in here who looked like he could kill—and just for the fun of it?

When he stepped closer again, I pressed my back into the wall behind me. "Relax. Name's Killer." My eyes widened and I whimpered. He cursed. "Club name," he muttered. He pointed to his vest, to one of the patches on it. "Just a club name. We're gonna get you out."

Fear vanished and agitation appeared. It had me up on my feet. "I can't. I told him I can't. No one else will get hurt because of me. Just go. Tell Ryan to get out and go. Please."

Only he wasn't listening to me. The shorts I had on came to my upper thighs. His eyes were there, and what I saw in them scared me. They'd hardened. His lips thinned and I could see his jaw clenching.

"Who did that?"

If I told him the truth, I had a feeling he would stalk upstairs and hurt Gloria on the spot. I couldn't let that happen. I didn't want anyone else involved; it only led to death.

"I did," I said quietly.

His eyes flashed to mine. "Lie."

How did he know? "N-no, I—"

"Don't bother." He shook his head. "We need to go and now."

"I won't," I told him. He didn't understand it, no one did, but I wasn't being some dim-witted teen. I was saving people.

"If you don't come willingly, I'll have to take you."

"Y-you can't." He took another step. I raised my hands in front of me. "Stop. Wait, please. You don't understand. If I stay, then no harm will come to my friend and her family."

"We'll protect them," he told me, his voice hard, and it made him sound like he believed what he'd said.

I shook my head, frustrated tears welling. "It's not that easy. If it was, I would have called the police on the phone I have." I flicked away the tear that fell. "Gloria knows people. If she's taken in, she'll still get a call out to take care of me, my friend, and her family. I won't risk more people."

He crossed his arms over his chest. "What do you mean by that? More people?"

I sucked in a shuddered breath. "T-they killed Donny and Mrs Minna, right in front of me, because of me. No more people will die," I said, steel in my voice.

"No one will. We have the means to protect you. Right now, we have the house surrounded. The four people upstairs will be taken into custody."

I gripped the hoodie at my chest. "Four?" I demanded.

"Yes. Four."

"Three men and one woman?" I asked. He nodded. Could it be *the* four? It had to be. They were the only ones who came to the house. The only voices I'd heard above and in my nightmares. Only I hadn't heard them that day, so I couldn't tell if it was the two other men I never wanted to see again.

I moved my hands down to my stomach when it twisted and growled. Killer's eyes hardened once again. Heat coloured my cheeks.

"T-they...." I wiped at my eyes. "They've killed, but they've also drugged and raped a girl. I-I saw her o-on the couch." His face blanked. I shook my head, curling my arms around my waist. My body shook like I'd been standing in the snow in my underwear for an hour. Frustration warred inside of me. This was my chance. I could be free, but I had to tell him everything. He nodded, wanting me to go on, but then he pulled his phone free and looked at the screen. He typed something back and then pocketed it again. "I…." I cleared my throat. "I think they've done it to more girls. Young girls. Maybe fourteen to sixteen. They're bad people. Bad."

He nodded. "How long you been down here?"

I looked away from him, to the floor, and whispered, "Over two years."

My eyes snapped up when I saw feet in front of me. I let out a strangled noise and backed against the wall, arms up.

"I won't hurt you."

"I-I can't trust anything."

He nodded once. "Smart." Slowly, he reached out and took my wrist. Gently, he used his other hand to slide up my sleeve. When he saw the scars, he cursed over and over. I pulled my arm from his hold.

He sucked in a deep breath through his nose. "Who did it?" he clipped. "You'll be safe no matter what, but we'll want to know."

"I'll be safe?"

He nodded.

I bit my bottom lip when it trembled. "Free from here, from them?"

His jaw clenched. "Yes."

Was I dreaming?

Could it really happen and I would be safe? Harriet and her family would be as well?

Noise rose above. Voices screamed, a door banged. More voices. I dropped to the floor in a crouch and covered my head.

Death.

Blood.

Failure.

Arms circled me. "You're good. You're fine. They're here to help."

"That bitch. That fucking bitch," rose above all other noises.

I cringed and burrowed my head into my knees more, tightened my arms around my head. I started humming when things got thrown around above, then whimpered when I heard the basement door fly open with a crash.

Banging footfalls rushed down. The arms around me dropped away. I felt him stand.

"Get up, bitch. Get the fuck up. They're dead. Do you hear me? Dead, just like you will be." A leg knocked into me. I whimpered and peeked to see Killer holding Gloria back.

More footsteps raced down the stairs.

"Get her the fuck outta here," Killer snarled.

"Warden, I'll take her," a man said. Hearing Ryan's last name, registering that time, I peeked out again to find Ryan standing just in front of Killer. Another man had a ranting Gloria by the arms and tugged her towards the stairs.

"I'll kill you, you pathetic bitch. You're dead."

They all ignored her. Ryan's eyes dropped to me. I lifted my head and watched Killer step close to Ryan. They shared quiet words. Ryan nodded before he turned and left the room.

My head swirled. He wanted nothing to do with me. I couldn't say I blamed him.

Killer turned to face me. "Come on, let's get you someplace safe."

"My friend Harriet White and her family. They need to be safe. She could still send someone for them."

"I'll let the right people know. She'll be fine." He walked closer, his hand held down and out for me. "Come on."

For the first time since being down there, I didn't want to leave because I didn't know what would happen next.

Still, I reached up and grabbed his hand, ready to take my chance of getting out of there, even when fear rattled my body.

CHAPTER FOURTEEN

EMERSON

*S*omeplace safe actually meant next door at Ryan's house. I didn't understand why Killer would lead me there, but he had. Then he planted me on the couch in the living room and stood beside it with his arms crossed over his chest. He looked menacing. If he hadn't been kind to me, I would be scared of him. Then again, I still was a little.

I pulled my legs up onto the couch and wrapped my arms around them. But then I thought better since my feet were still only covered in socks and the walk there could have dirtied them. I didn't want to leave any marks on Ryan's couch, so I placed them back on the floor. I arranged the hoodie so it covered the marks on my thighs and then tucked my hands under my knees, hunching in on myself.

When Killer had led me from the house and through the front door, no one had been around. I had heard voices coming from the back rooms in the house—where I kept peering over my shoulder to make sure no one was coming after me—but we'd made it safely into Ryan's. As I sat there, I glanced around for the first time.

The living room had the basic needs. Some furniture was still covered, which made me think Ryan had been painting recently. The couch I sat on faced the front door, and I surreptitiously glanced there and then away. There were stairs to the right of the couch.

Stairs.

They made me think of Mrs Minna and the lie Gloria had made up. My eyes stayed riveted to the bottom of the stairs where Lenny would have laid her body.

My stomach heaved. I covered my mouth and coughed.

Killer looked down at me. I quickly moved my gaze to my knees, tucking my hand back under.

"You need anythin'? Water? Food? Blanket?"

I shook my head, even when I could use all of those. "No," I whispered. I wouldn't be more of a problem for him or Ryan than I already was.

Flashing lights shined through the front windows. The police had arrived. "A-are you sure Harriet and her family will be all right?" I asked again.

"We've got someone at the address you gave us."

I nodded. "Thank you."

He made a noise in the back of his throat; it almost sounded like a growl. "Don't need to thank us."

I nodded again. "Okay," I whispered.

"You wanna tell me who gave you those scars yet?"

Did I?

Honestly, I wished he'd never seen them.

"Gloria."

He cursed. "Your aunt, right?"

"Yes."

Before he could say anything, we heard footsteps, a lot of them on the front porch. Reacting, I hunched over more. My blood pumped faster through my veins. When the door burst open, I let out a squeak, then spotted Ryan stepping through. More men followed. My chest ached at seeing them all. They looked big, angry, and intimidating.

But then I heard a woman's voice behind them all, snapping and cursing.

"No," I whispered. "She's here," I cried. I moved so fast my head spun. I was up and over the back of the couch, curling in on myself, hiding. They didn't take her. She'd sweetened her way around them. They believed her.

She'd kill me.

Kill Harriet.

"It's not her. It's not your aunt," Killer said, crouched at my side. The woman said something. Hearing her harsh voice had me whimpering. She could hurt me like Gloria did. I knew, deep down, it wasn't logical, but I couldn't stop the fear clogging my throat.

"Violet, out," I thought I heard Ryan say.

Killer disappeared from beside me, but then I heard him. "She's not good with women. Her aunt abused her. She's got scars—"

A sob caught my throat, and the voices in the room stilled.

"Come on, sweetheart. We'll wait outside," a man said to the woman named Violet.

"I don't think she's good with a bunch of us in here," Killer added.

"Call him. No women, but him," Ryan said. His voice was clear and familiar. "Give the room to Lan, me, and Killer."

I listened to people leave and waited. I suddenly felt foolish for freaking out. They'd helped me, were keeping my friend safe. They'd gotten me out, and here I was on the floor, my legs tucked up under my hoodie, hiding behind a couch all because a group of men and a woman's voice scared me.

When the door closed, Ryan said, "We'll wait for him before

you question her." No one replied, but the message must have been accepted because the room fell silent.

It was after some time, after I sat there wallowing for being a coward and regretting acting the way I had, that I offered, "I'm sorry."

Someone grunted.

Killer, who'd been standing beside me, eyes into the living room, glanced down at me. "What'd I say about sayin' sorry?"

Drawing in a shuddering breath, I said, "Not to."

"Damn right. You just stay there and relax, yeah?"

I nodded, unsure who we were waiting for, but I had the need to stand and look at Ryan. I hadn't seen him up close, with his eyes actually on me, but then I was scared with how he would take me in. I looked like I'd crawled from the sewers. I probably even smelled like it. Shame had me staying where I was.

My body jolted when there was a knock. I didn't hear anyone move, but I heard the door open and then, "Hello, my hunky men. I'm here ready for duty. Where do you want me? And someone please say the bedroom."

Someone cursed, there was a groan, and I saw Killer looking at the floor, clenching his teeth, and shaking his head. Who was the man who could say something like that to burly men and get away with it?

"Julian, just get over there," Ryan said.

"Oh, I get it. You want to watch me walk. Some foreplay first," he teased, his voice coming closer my way. "I like the way you think. Why I bet—why, hello there, my dove." The man in jeans and a polo tee got to his knees at the end of the couch. His smile was warm, just like his eyes. "My name's Julian. I'm a friend of these divine creatures…."

I knew right away why they called Julian in. Already my shoulders eased and my stomach unclenched. His smile was infectious. I wanted to smile with him, yet I didn't. The man felt like sunshine on a cold, miserable day.

"Emerson," I said.

"Emerson." His smile grew. "Such a pretty name for a cutie pie. How about I find you a shower and a change of clothes. Then we can have a chat with the sexy cop over there." I glanced the way he thumbed, but all I saw was the couch.

A shower sounded amazing though. But I hated the thought of making the police officer wait more than he already had.

"I've wasted time. I should—"

His hand shot up. I flinched, and his smile dimmed a little. He lowered his hand to his thigh. "Don't you worry about the men here. They won't care about waiting until you have a nice warm shower."

Did that mean I did stink?

My cheeks warmed. "Okay," I said meekly. I dipped my eyes down to the floor. Julian's hand slowly came into view. I pulled my head up. He tapped my hand.

"Let's get you upstairs."

It meant standing. It meant walking by Ryan and the officer, Lan. It meant going near and then up the stairs. The ones where I knew Mrs Minna's body had been.

But moving meant living. It meant being strong and finding who I used to be again.

Maybe with a shower, a real shower after years, I could get one step closer to me.

I slid my hand in his. Julian's smile softened. He stood and gently pulled me up with him. I made sure my thighs were covered. I wasn't strong yet, so I kept my eyes on the floor as Julian led me towards the stairs.

My hand gripped Julian's tightly. When we reached the bottom of the stairs, my eyes watered, I sucked in a harsh breath, but I kept going. I kept moving and stopped myself from thinking of Mrs Minna.

Before we reached the second-floor landing, Julian called down, "Do one of you handsome men want to find some clothes for my dove?"

"I-I have clothes next door."

His lips thinned for a fraction of a second, and I had a feeling he'd somehow seen my clothes next door in the basement.

"Don't you stress, pet. They'll find something." He tucked my hand into his elbow and patted it. "Let's conquer this shower, get you all toasty and warm." He walked us into a bathroom that was down a hall, off a sitting area at the top of the stairs. His hands dropped away when he went over to the shower and turned on the water. "You know, I prefer a bath, but my man loves his showers."

"Your man?" I blurted. I should have guessed he was gay; he was very flamboyant, but I didn't want to presume and be wrong.

"Oh yes, honey. He's my one and only. Even though I tease him greatly about the other men we hang out with, I'm devoted to my poppet. Besides, a little jealousy spices up the bedroom, if you know what I mean?"

I shook my head. I meant to say I did know what he meant because I understood it, but I'd never felt it.

"Not to worry, my dove. You'll know one day. I'm sure of it."

I doubted it, but I didn't say so. Not with the scars on my body. No one would want to stare at them. I didn't even want to look at them and they were on my body.

"Oh." Julian's gasp had me looking at him. His eyes were on my arm. I glanced down. Absently, I'd been rubbing my fingers over the scars on my arm.

My stomach bottomed out. I hated that Killer had seen them. I'd even kept my shorts hanging low so I could cover the ones on my thighs because I hadn't wanted Julian to see them. They were dirty and ugly. He was light and sweet.

I pulled both sleeves down and gripped them in my fists, bringing them up under my arms.

Julian shook his head at me. "My dove," he whispered.

Tears pooled in my eyes.

He stepped right up to me, and I was proud I didn't retreat. His eyes were too kind for me to back away. Gently, he tucked my hair behind my ear before dropping his hands to the bottom of my hoodie. Slowly, he lifted.

If it had been anyone else, I would have freaked. I would have fought. I would have pushed. But with Julian, I let him lift the hoodie from my body. He gazed at my arms and my scarred chest in the low-cut tee.

Sadness filled me. Tears dropped from my eyes. "Do you see?" I whispered. "No one will want this."

His bottom lip wobbled, his eyes welling. "Oh, honey, no." He ran his hands up and down my arms. I wanted to move away from his touch, but he said, "I see a woman who is strong. Who has lived through hell and has come out on the other side. I know someone will love you for who you are, not what they see, because you are beautiful."

A sob caught in my dry throat. I tipped forward, my forehead landing against his chest as I let out a keening sound. His arms wrapped around me, holding me tightly against him as I cried.

He kept holding me, whispering words of praise, until I could pull myself together.

Straightening, I winced. Julian saw it and asked, "Are you okay?"

I snorted. I wasn't sure if I'd ever be.

He amended, "Are you hurt?"

"My ribs are tender. S-she kicked me." Up until then, since the adrenaline had worn off, I hadn't thought or reacted to the twinge in my ribs.

Julian hummed under his breath, his smile tight. "My mother-in-law is a nurse. She could come by and check."

"No!" I cried. My pulse throbbed from how fast it raced. I took a deep breath. "Sorry, but please, no nurse."

"Honey." His gaze ran over me again, and then he said softly, "You could be malnourished, need medical treatment."

I grabbed his wrist. "Please, please no doctors, no nurses, and no women. I promise I'll eat, I'll drink, and I'll get better."

His lips thinned, but eventually he nodded. "I'll see if they need wrapping after the shower." He leaned in and kissed my temple, something my father used to do. "Take your time."

"Thank you," I said as he walked towards the door.

"No thanks needed. I'll put fresh clothes outside the door. No one will be up here, okay?"

I nodded and offered up a wonky smile.

When he closed the door after he left, the smile dropped from my mouth. I took a steadying breath and removed the clothes I hoped to never see again. A moment later, I stepped under the spray of water. The temperature was perfect, and I sighed contently.

My mind ran through the events.

I was out.

Free.

I still couldn't believe it. There would be moments when I wouldn't feel safe, sure they'd come back for me somehow. I was certain of it. But right then, happiness started to form throughout my body.

No more Gloria.

No more Lenny.

Or two meals a day.

Or wearing ratty clothes.

I didn't know where or if they'd left any money from my father's accounts, but I would deal with that later.

I was out.

Away from that hellhole.

Elation had my chest expanding, a giddy laugh falling free while my stomach spun. I lifted my head into the pouring warm water and smiled.

CHAPTER FIFTEEN

WARDEN

*W*hen Emmie cleared the stairs and we heard the bathroom door open, I looked to Lan and Killer. We all wore weary and worried expressions. A shiver of anger ran over my body. I wanted to rip those cunts a new arsehole.

When I saw the basement, how she'd been living for *two years*.... Christ, ripping them a new one hadn't been my only thought. I pulled the notebook we'd found out of my back pocket and handed it to Lan.

"She wrote about her experience." My jaw clenched. I'd read the first part and murder had been on my mind. They'd killed the guy she went on one date with. Right in front of her. She'd seen a girl on the couch, drugged out and raped. Marshalling my calm, I sucked in a deep breath. "I didn't read it all, but what I did was enough to make sure none of them see the light of day for a very fuckin' long time." Lan turned to the pictures she drew—ones that were clear as day at identifying who they were. Bloody perfect. I pointed to one. "All except him. We don't know who this one is yet. What we don't have is a picture of the drug supplier who was there tonight. My guess is Emmie's never seen him before."

Lan nodded. "He's been wanted for a hell of a long time. He'll go away for an extended period as well."

"This situation is fucked up."

"Even worse, another thing I caught in there"—I pointed at the book—"was that those motherfucking cunts are connected to drugging, kidnapping, and raping women before they get dumped with no memory. It's how all this shit started for her. She walked in on the cunts filmin' a girl drugged out on the couch and getting fucked. They freaked, killed the guy Emmie had been with, and locked her in the basement."

"Jesus Christ. Fucking hell," Lan muttered. He snapped the book closed, rolled it, and put it in his back pocket. "When I get her recorded interview, that and the book will be iron-clad proof for the case. Like you said, they'll be going away for a long time."

I nodded. This whole situation was fucked. It had my gut coiling in revulsion. "At least my client will have answers as well," I muttered, more to myself than the others.

"We have your client's statement on file. I'll add it to what we get off Emerson," Lan said, then added, "Do you know why Emerson was freaked about Vi?"

"Not Violet," Killer supplied. He leaned his arse on the arm of the couch. "It was more her voice, and the fact that she's female. I think she'll have to be watched around any woman. The aunt did a number on her."

"What do you mean?" I clipped.

"You might not have seen them. Her thighs looked like they'd been sliced up with knives. I got a peek of her wrist and it looked the same. Her cunt of an aunt did it to her. I don't know what else she's done, but fuck, to live through that would be enough nightmares for decades."

"It's not only her thighs and wrist," Julian said. We watched him descend the stairs, and when he stopped at the bottom, he went on, "Her full arms and chest as well. Currently, she might have cracked or bruised ribs. All from her aunt. I suggested we call Nancy, but she won't have it. She doesn't even want to go to the hospital to get checked out."

Fury rang in my ears. Murder wouldn't be enough for fucking Gloria. She needed pain, slowly, and for the rest of her life.

"Can't say I blame her for not wanting Nancy near her right now," Killer said.

Julian sighed and then nodded. "I'll wrap her after the shower just in case. She's only wincing, so I'm thinking they're more bruised than cracked."

I didn't like the thought of Julian near her like that. Not that I understood completely why, but it chafed me the wrong way.

Yet I ignored it. I wouldn't look like a dickhead saying shit and stopping Julian from helping Emmie.

"Where's she gonna stay?" Killer asked.

"She can stay here," I volunteered without even thinking, then snapped my mouth shut knowing it was wrong. They all looked at me. "Actually, she should stay with you, Julian. She seems comfortable."

He smiled. "Isn't everyone."

"Nope," Lan said.

"No," Killer clipped.

"Not really," I admitted.

Julian rolled his eyes. "Stop it, you'll make me blush. I know you all love me. But you're right, Loki. She should stay with me and Mattie. I'll see if I can get her to talk to someone professionally as well, but it's also doubtful." He dragged out his phone from his pocket. "I'll ring my man now and let him know."

"I'll head out and talk to the rest. Get Vi to grab her change of clothes from the car for Emmie."

Julian winked. Lan and Killer gave me a chin lift. Before turning, I caught Julian heading into the kitchen to call Mattie. I went out the front, closing the door behind me. On the porch and lawn stood Violet, Travis, Butch, Talon, Griz, Blue, and Stoke.

"How is she?" Violet asked. She moved closer. Travis was right behind her, curling an arm over her chest for her to rest back against him.

"You got that spare change of clothes in the car?" I asked.

She nodded. "I'll get it." Someone must have gone to get her car because it was parked alongside another couple of cars and Harleys.

I waited until she was back and had placed the folded items in my hands before continuing. "You all know I found a book Emmie had written while in the basement. Those fuckers will be going away for a damn long time for the evidence she's given." I met Violet's eyes. "They're the ones involved in kidnapping, drugging, and raping the young girls. Worse, what I read was that the events had been recorded. They probably sell them on the black market."

"But how is she?" Violet pressed.

"Not good." I glanced at my feet, shaking my head. Once more, the fury resurfaced inside of me. "She witnessed two people get murdered. Blamed herself for them." Understanding dawned in Violet's eyes. That was why Emmie didn't want anyone else to get hurt. "She's afraid of women right now because her motherfucking aunt did a job on her. She has bruised ribs from being kicked. She has scars lining her thighs, arms, and chest. The woman cut her own niece. Sliced her up."

Curses went up around me.

I cleared my throat. "I have to get these clothes back in. Julian's done his magic and got her in the shower, and she'll be going to stay at his place. There was a picture of a guy in the book of Emmie's we don't know. If he's heard about the shit going down, she's better to stay close to the compound."

Talon spoke up. "I'll have the brothers rotate shifts, keeping an eye on the place."

"That'd be good."

"We'll peel out. Get it sorted now. Tell Killer to escort Emmie to Julian and Mattie's."

"Done." I went to go back inside as Talon and his crew left, when Violet called my name.

I turned back. She got close. Her voice was soft, quiet. "You sure she wouldn't be better here?"

I ground my teeth together.

"You have a system that no one could break into. She knows you more than Julian."

"She's not stayin' here. She's comfortable with Julian."

"She is with you as well."

"I haven't been around her for more than a minute." And yet, I wanted to talk to her more. I wanted to fucking hug her, but I didn't. I also ignored the fact that I'd lost my breath when I first saw her. Attraction had slammed into me so damn hard, I'd had to quickly walk away from the basement. Away from her. It was the right thing to do. She looked twenty, tops, but her eyes said she was so much older. None of it mattered though. The texting, the small connection. Staying away from Emerson was the best option.

"Yet you and her have been talking over text for a while."

I shook my head. "She didn't text back. She refused help." She was probably pissed I'd butted in, but it had to be done. For her and the others. She'd accept it one day.

"But—"

"Vi, enough. She's stayin' with Julian and Mattie. She'll be safe there until we get this last guy. Then she can be wherever she wants to be."

Violet searched my face, saw my resolve, sighed and nodded. "Okay. Get Lan to send a picture and whatever he has back from the school about the girl there. Butch and I'll hit the office bright and early to help work on it."

I grunted, flicked a wave to Butch and Travis, and then went back inside. Julian was on me as soon as I stepped inside, taking the clothes and heading up the stairs.

I caught Killer's gaze. "Talon wants you to escort them to Julian's house since we don't know who that fourth guy is just yet." He nodded once. I looked to Lan. "Vi's askin' for the photo of the guy that Emmie drew, and if you get anything from your source at the school to let her know. They're gonna do their own diggin'."

"All right." He ran a hand through his hair. "Glad you called me in on this, Warden. They need to be behind bars."

"They'd better suffer in there." I didn't like the choice of calling Lan in, but Violet had gone above me and done it.

"They will," Killer clipped. "Hawks'll make sure of it."

At least there was that.

A creak from above had me glancing towards the stairs. Julian appeared. He was smiling behind him as he descended. My mouth dried at the first sight of Emmie. She was smiling softly down at Julian. Her eyes had life to them, her cheeks colour, her hair wet but clean.

She looked damn beautiful.

The clothes I'd given over had been a tee and jeans from Violet. The tee poked out the top of a hoodie she'd put on. My hoodie. It swam on her. Even the jeans looked a little big. Shit, I wanted to go into the kitchen and make her a meal.

Fuck it.

Turning, I stalked into the kitchen and took out some bread, sliced turkey, and cheese. I made a quick sandwich, then poured her a glass of cold water. I could hear Lan's gentle voice talking with Emmie.

Picking up the plate and glass, I went back into the living room. First, I saw the back of Emmie's head. She sat on the couch with Julian beside her. Killer at her back. Lan sat on the coffee table in front of her. He stopped talking when he saw me. His lips twitched for some reason and he pulled back when I got close.

I held out the plate and glass. "Food. Water. Eat. Drink."

Killer snorted behind her. Emmie stared down at the items, up at me, and then down again. Julian chuckled, as did Lan. Thank fuck Emmie slowly held out her hand for the plate and took it. Julian grabbed the glass for her.

"Thank you," she whispered. She put the plate on her lap and tucked her arm around it, like she thought someone would take it from her.

What she didn't do was eat it.

I hovered over her, waiting.

After a moment, she glanced up. I met her gaze, then looked down to the plate and back up to her lips.

Bad mistake.

They were plumped and wet from her licking them.

Christ.

I backed up near the stairs, crossing my arms over my chest. I kept my gaze on Lan, who cleared his throat, covered his laugh with a cough, and started talking again.

Out the corner of my eye, I caught Emmie picking up half of her sandwich and taking a small bite, nodding at something Lan said.

Fuck. I scrubbed a hand over my face and ignored Julian's

bright smile aimed at me. I looked back to Lan, tuning in on what he said.

"—they won't get offered bond. They'll keep them in because of all the incriminating charges. Then with your pictures and everything you've written, we'll be able to find the other guy." He pointed to the man we didn't know in Emmie's book.

The colour drained from her cheeks. She dropped the sandwich to the plate and pressed both of her hands down on her stomach.

I wanted to punch Lan in the throat.

"He's still out there—" Her mouth snapped closed and she thinned her lips.

Julian rubbed her back. "They'll find him. You'll be safe. You don't have to worry. You know Lan's a cop, Warden's a private investigator"—her eyes flicked to me—"and Killer's part of the Hawks MC." She looked back at Killer, who nodded. "You're well protected. You'll come home with me"—when her eyes widened and looked to me again, I bit my tongue to stop from shouting that she was staying—"and Mattie and I live across the road from the Hawks MC compound."

"We'll be rotating shifts to keep an eye out," Killer said. "No one will get to you."

"What about Harriet?"

"We'll have her house and whereabouts covered as well," Killer replied.

Lan smiled softly at her. "You don't have anything to worry about."

Finally she nodded, but I could see how tense her body was locked. She didn't believe him. How could she trust after what she'd been through?

"Do you think you could answer some questions, Emerson?" Lan asked.

"Yes," she whispered.

Fucking hell, she needed more food, rest, and some damn peaceful sleep. I knew she wouldn't get it until this last dick-head was found. Even then, nightmares would still plague her. Why did I want to wrap her up and hide her away from everything that could hurt her?

CHAPTER SIXTEEN

EMERSON

*A*s I told the officer, Lan Davis, everything I knew and everything I went through, my mind replayed his words over and over. Each time it tore at my belly.

There was one still out there.

One Gloria could contact to hunt me or Harriet down.

I wasn't safe. Not yet.

She could tell him Ryan's part of the night. He could be after Ryan.

Ryan, who hadn't really looked at me since sitting there. Ryan, who had made me a drink and a sandwich. Ryan, who I couldn't stop glancing at out the corner of my eye. What would he think when hearing everything? I couldn't read his reaction; his face was a blank mask as he watched Lan question me.

"T-that's everything I know," I said. Julian squeezed my arm. I glanced at him with a grateful smile. He'd been amazing. I'd be leaving Ryan's house to stay at Julian's. But I didn't want to. Everything in me demanded I stay right there, but I wouldn't. Julian was being kind enough to take me in, so I wouldn't decline it.

It seemed Ryan had thought it'd be best, or he would have gotten me to stay there with him. Right? I thought he might have, but his blank face didn't react when Julian said I'd be going home with him and Mattie.

It wasn't that I didn't appreciate the offer. God, I was so very grateful for Julian. So much so I could cry. Only, I just… it was strange and crazy, but I felt safer with Ryan. My heart told me he was familiar.

But I wouldn't stay where I wasn't wanted.

Not that I knew he didn't want me there.

I rubbed at my temples. The headache beating at my brain grew worse with all the thinking.

Lan's hand touched my knee, and I jumped. He took it away quickly.

Ryan cursed, but before I could look at him, Lan spoke. "Thank you. That's more than enough."

I nodded. Exhaustion had taken hold, so I blinked lazily at him.

"She needs sleep," Ryan stated, moving from his position near the stairs. He came forward, held out his hand to Lan. "Keep me posted."

Lan took his hand and shook it. "I will." Lan stood, and he looked down at me. "You'll be okay," he told me, and I wasn't sure I had an answer because I didn't know if I would be.

It counted that I was free. Boy, did it count. It helped me breathe easier.

But the nightmares I knew would follow kept my mind mixed up.

My body ached, my head swam, but a lot of it felt like it was coming from the thought of leaving Ryan Warden.

It was dangerous to have that reaction. Especially when I wasn't enough for a man such as him. Someone rugged, smart, handsome, nice, demanding, and sweet.

Julian squeezed my hand. I glanced at him, and he said, "Are you ready to go, my dove?"

I nodded. Julian stood and helped me up with him.

Lan started for the door first, then Killer, Julian, me, and finally Ryan. I wanted to glance over my shoulder. Wanted to talk to him, or even tell him thank you again for his kindness. I opened my mouth, closed it, and thought, *just say something.*

On the porch out front, Lan turned to me. "I'll be sure to check in every day," he said.

"Thank you for... being nice."

His jaw clenched. He nodded and glanced at Ryan before taking off to his car. Julian stepped down the front steps, and since my hand was in his, I followed.

"Emmie," Ryan called softly, causing my heart to jump extra quick.

I pulled my hand free and faced him. His palm was held out my way. I glanced down to see he held my phone. With a trembling hand, I reached out and took it. I crushed it to my chest.

Slowly, I looked up. His expression was blank, but his eyes held something more. I didn't understand what. Licking my dry lips, I whispered, "Thank you.... You, um.... Just, thank you." *For everything.*

He didn't reply, just kept his gaze connected with mine and then eventually tilted his chin up at me. I noticed a tick in his jaw. I watched it for a moment, wondering why it did that.

"Emmie, honey," Julian said.

I glanced over my shoulder at him. He tipped his head towards the car. The vehicle looked so far away.

Away from Ryan.

Coldness soaked into my bones. My body shivered. They stood around waiting on me, and yet I couldn't seem to turn fully and leave.

But I had to.

Drawing in a deep breath, I nodded to Julian. Glancing back at Ryan, I peeked up at him through my lashes. "Goodbye," I muttered.

Thank you again, and I'm sorry for darkening your days.

He grunted, "Later."

It was then that I knew I had to move. He said no more, and I didn't know exactly what I waited for. So I turned back to Julian. He gave me a closed-lip smile and held out his hand. I took it, and we made our way to the car where Killer stood with his motorcycle.

I wrapped my free arm around my waist. When Julian dropped my hand to open the passenger door, I used that hand to grip the hoodie at my chest because it had started to ache.

"Let's go," Julian said cheerily.

Don't look back. Don't look back.

I looked back. Ryan stood on the porch, leaning against the wall just to the side of the house. Since it was dark, I couldn't make out his expression. My betraying bottom lip trembled. I quickly bit down on it.

He had been a part of my days for so long.

I didn't want to go.

I didn't want to walk away from him.

"Hey," Julian whispered. My body jolted and I faced him. He smiled sadly. "You can go back to him. He won't mind you staying there."

Roughly, I wiped my eyes. "No, I'm okay." That part of my life was over. I had a feeling it included Ryan Warden as well, and that hurt me more than the scars Gloria inflicted.

Sighing, I quickly slid into the car and didn't look back out. Julian closed the door. Killer started his bike as Julian came around the car and got in. He started it, and out the corner of my eye, I caught him wave.

I didn't look.

Too afraid I'd get out of the car and run back to Ryan, begging him to let me stay by his side. Too worried I would burst into tears.

Ryan had been a part of my life for over two months. He'd been my distraction and my lifeline, and inevitably, my attraction to him had grown.

Had it grown into something that I never should have felt? Possibly.

But I wouldn't change it. I knew the type of man he was, and he deserved to have my affection. Even if he didn't know about it.

The car moved away. I gripped my phone tighter and clenched my jaw to stop from saying anything. I closed my eyes to keep the tears behind them. My stomach churned, my pulse raced, and the back of my neck broke out in a sweat. I tapped my feet to the floor in a nervous patter.

"Are you okay?" Julian groaned at his own question. "I mean... Warden and you, something happened?"

Snorting, I opened my eyes, only to have them water. I wiped them away jerkily. "No." I shook my head. More tears fell. "Only...." I shrugged, then winced when my side twinged. I glanced out the window. "He... was next door and...." I puffed out an annoyed breath.

"I think I get it," Julian said. "You've had him next door for a while. You're used to him. From what I heard, you two talked a little."

I shrugged again. "Just a little." My eyes drifted down to my phone.

"Well, you know he'll only be a phone call away."

"I wouldn't call him."

I could feel Julian's eyes on me as we stopped at a red light. The rumble of Killer's bike had me looking out the window again to see him next to us. He gave me a nod. I waved lamely.

"Why?" Julian asked when we drove off again.

"He's done enough. He doesn't need me pestering him." Did that sound whiny? I wasn't sure, but the words rang true. Ryan didn't need someone like me in his life.

"I don't think he'd agree with that," Julian said as he pulled into a driveway. I glanced out the back window to see Killer behind us. He climbed off his bike. Julian went on when he turned off the car. "Warden isn't built like that. He cares. He may seem gruff, but he has a heart of a big squishy teddy bear. A lot of the men in our family and group of friends do." He looked out the windscreen and his smile grew. "Speaking of teddy bears, there's mine."

A man who looked younger than Julian walked towards the car. He had a small smile on his lips, but it widened when Julian waved crazily.

At least Julian was distracted from our previous conversation. He was sweet to say Ryan wouldn't agree with my thoughts. Even if that was the case, I couldn't ring Ryan. I had to distance myself from him. For my own sake.

Julian's door popped open, and the man stuck his head in. "Hey," he greeted Julian, his eyes raking all over him and softening.

"Hi, poppet," Julian cooed. He grabbed the man's chin, kissed him quickly, and then moved his face to look at me. "Look what I found. A dove. My dove, this is my better half, Mathew. But his friends call him Mattie. Poppet, this is our Emmie."

"Hey, Emmie."

"Hi, Mattie." We both laughed.

It felt foreign coming out of my mouth, but I had a feeling many people laughed around Julian.

Something hit the roof of the car, and I let out a squeak.

Mattie was pushed back, and Killer's face appeared. "Sorry," he bit out.

"It's all right," I told him. It was my fault for being so jumpy. "Let's get inside, yeah?"

"Aye, aye, captain," Julian called, then saluted. Killer sighed and disappeared out the door. Mattie walked around the car, came to my side, and opened my door.

He stepped back. I unclicked my seat belt, gripped my phone, and climbed out of the car. Julian was in front of us, saying, "Come on, let's get you settled."

He always seemed so energetic and happy. I wondered if he'd always been like that. He held the front door open to a cute weatherboard house. Mattie came up behind me and explained, "This used to be my sister's house. But when Zara and Talon got hitched, she moved out to live with him and the kids in his home. It's small, just two bedrooms, but Julian and I love it."

"That we do." Julian curled an arm around Mattie's shoulders and tugged him close. "You'll have a room right next to ours. Just ignore the moaning—" Mattie slapped a hand over Julian's mouth. When Mattie turned red, laughter bubbled out of me.

Honestly, it was no wonder they called Julian into situations. He was amazing.

"He means snoring. Ignore the snoring that he does all on his own," Mattie said.

Julian rolled his eyes as he grabbed Mattie's hand and pulled it down. "That's right, poppet."

"Before you show her the room to crash in," Killer said. When he had my eyes, he went on, "I'll be around. If it's not me patrolling outside, it'll be one of my brothers. They'll all have the same club vest, different patches, but the same one. If any of you see someone without a vest, call the club."

"We will," Mattie replied.

"Not our first rodeo, cowboy," Julian said.

Killer's jaw clenched. He nodded, turned, and walked out of the house.

"Thank you," I called. He waved over his shoulder.

Julian came up beside me and put his arm around me while Mattie closed the front door and locked it. "Don't you worry about those biker guys. They don't talk much, and when they do, they sound like cavemen, but they're the best kind of men there are. Well, besides me and my poppet."

I believed him. They all seemed to be willing to help me, no matter what.

Julian hugged me to his side. "Come check out your room."

Your room.

He hadn't said their spare room but *your* room.

Already they treated me as if I was a part of their group. Appreciation swelled inside of me. I hadn't felt kindness in such a long time.

Julian led me down the hall with Mattie following. He chatted the whole way while ignoring my tears and wobbly bottom lip.

As Julian told me about where I could find things, Mattie stepped up close. He bumped his shoulder into mine. "Are you okay?" he whispered.

Wiping at my face, I told him, "I think I will be." Especially once the fourth man was behind bars like the rest of those foul, hurtful, disgusting people.

CHAPTER SEVENTEEN

EMERSON

A scream tore out of my mouth. I opened my eyes and blinked quickly into the room. A room I was becoming very familiar with since it had been mine for a month. Dimly lit from the night light I had plugged into the power point below the window, I tried to control my breathing. I focussed on the small light, appreciating it as much as I despised it. What adult needed a darn night light?

My door burst open and Julian stumbled in. At least he was clothed. The first night I'd woken, screaming from a nightmare —the first evening in their home—Julian raced in sporting a naked body and a baseball bat.

"Where, where?" he'd shouted, turning this way and that.

Mattie had appeared next, holding a knife, though he wore boxers. "What is it?" he asked. Within seconds, he'd taken in the room, seen no threat, and guessed, "Nightmare?"

I'd nodded with my hand over my eyes.

"Oh, my poor dove. Julian's here for you." The bed had dipped. I'd gasped, opened my eyes, and found Julian climbing on the bed.

Mattie had grabbed his shoulders and pulled him from it. "Okay, hero, how about you get dressed first or let me handle this?"

His eyes had widened as he glanced down at himself, covering his junk and chuckling. "Sorry about that. Bet you'll have nice dreams now."

Mattie had once again grabbed his shoulders and turned him towards the door.

With a shove, he ordered, "Go. I've got this."

"I know, my poppet. Night, night, dovey dove," Julian called before disappearing.

"Ah… goodnight," I replied.

Mattie had tiredly run a hand over his face. He'd glanced at me, and we'd both started laughing. He'd made his way to the bed and lay on the blankets. He told me of the first time he met Julian. How freaked out he'd been because he'd been so attracted to Julian though he hadn't even come out to anyone. He told me about Julian and what his parents were like. My heart had splintered and then cracked for the wonderful man. Never would I have thought Julian had been through something so devastating because of how he was now. He'd just proven to me that things could get better if we had the right people in our lives, and because he was strong. I wasn't sure if I could be that strong, but I wanted to try. I'd cried, sometimes talked, but Mattie did the most of it. Until I'd drifted off to sleep once more.

After the first night, my waking from fright happened so often that either Julian or Mattie would come to bed with me, and when I woke, because I always woke, they would lull me back to sleep with stories.

That was until I told them it had to stop. I was already in their house, interrupting their time together. I wouldn't burden their sleep by having them become my security blanket.

"You okay?" Julian asked.

I groaned, flopping back to the mattress. "This is becoming too much. I have to move out."

He stomped into the room, his hands moving to his hips. "Now you stop that. My dove is allowed to have nightmares because she was in a fucked-up situation."

"Every night for the last month?"

"Yes, dammit," he snapped. "Don't be hard on yourself, Emmie. I won't let you."

I hit the mattress with my fist. It was just so frustrating. I was away from them, from that house. I had beautiful, kind friends with Julian and Mattie. They made sure I always had what I wanted. Julian didn't mind at all using my bank card Violet, Ryan's boss, had found in Gloria's purse. Especially since I surprisingly had enough in the account to make sure I didn't go without until I turned twenty-five.

I had nothing to complain about.... Well, except for the matter of Phillip Burrows. He was the main player in his and Gloria's little setup of selling their rape videos on the black market. Unfortunately, by the time Lan found out who he was, Burrows had already taken off, disappearing from his family and friends. All connections. Gloria must have gotten word to him about what had happened. We didn't know if he was overseas by now, or waiting in a corner to fulfil Gloria's wishes to make me pay. How we'd found his name was from the girl who'd been attending a school pretending to be me. She was his niece. Her mother, Phillip's sister, had been addicted to meth and threatened her daughter to go through with it to keep her supply of drugs coming in. The girl had been taken into protective custody in case her uncle or mother, who was in jail, went after her for some reason.

Somehow, they'd managed to keep the whole case out of public record for now, but the families of all involved had been notified and asked not to go public with it yet. There was something about an ongoing sting operation. I didn't really understand, but that was fine. I was just relieved. I didn't want people to know what had happened to me. I hadn't even reached out to Harriet. I felt terrible for not wanting to speak with her, but I wasn't ready for it and all the questions that would come. Then again, Julian told me I shouldn't have felt too bad because she hadn't come looking for me either, and she knew what I'd been through.

People still freaked me out. Especially large crowds and women. It had been a couple of days later when there was a knock at the door. My body had reacted, but mainly because I'd thought it could be Ryan. It still held out some type of expectation that Ryan would come and want to spend time with me. I'd ignored my dancing belly and watched Julian open the front door. There were a group of women standing there. My throat had closed over as a shiver had torn through me. I'd jumped up and run from the room like the coward I was.

Julian had come in later and told me that had been Mattie's sister and her crew. While he'd assured me they were nice women, I couldn't bring myself to meet them.

"It's okay, my dove. They understand, and I do too. When you're ready, you can meet them. Maybe one at a time."

I'd nodded, and he'd hugged me close, then left the room.

I'd felt like a complete moron and had wanted to rush back out there and meet them, act normal and happy and safe... but I hadn't been able to move from the bed.

Maybe one day that would change. All I had to do was wait for it.

I hoped it was soon.

"You're thinking too hard," Julian commented from the

doorway. The hallway light was on so I squinted, allowing my eyes to adjust.

"Why are you dressed?"

He laughed. "I'm not a nudist yet, Emmie. I do like clothes."

I sat up and shook my head. "No. I mean, why are you dressed at—" I lit up my phone on the bedside table. "—one o'clock. You and Mattie are like granddads. You're always in bed early like me. Why are you awake?"

He sighed, then came all the way in and sat on the bed next to me. He grabbed my phone and started fiddling with it. "We had a visitor," he mumbled.

My heart skipped a beat and I tensed. "Who?"

He didn't answer right away, and it caused my pulse to race. Julian glanced at me, passing my phone. I took it without looking at it.

His eyes widened. "No one bad," he reassured and curled me into his side with an arm around my shoulders. I didn't understand why it was so easy for me to receive affection from Julian and Mattie, but I was grateful for it. "It's okay, dovey dove. Nothing bad."

"Then who would come here so late?"

"Warden."

"Ryan," I whispered, and it sounded like I was shocked by a magical creature. In a way, I guessed Ryan was one. I hadn't seen him since leaving his house that night. All I knew was that he'd been working the case. More recently he was out searching for Phillip Burrows.

Other than that information, I'd heard nothing.

Messaging him never strayed far from my mind, but I stuck to my guns and didn't. I was sure my phone was getting worn down by the number of times I looked at our exchanged messages though. I hadn't seen his last one until I opened it the day after getting to Julian's.

But Ryan had been here. Why?

I cleared my throat. "Um… what was he here for?"

Julian played with my hair, twirling it around and through his fingers. I loved it when he did that. He seemed to know it relaxed me, because I started to settle into him more.

"He popped in to see how you were."

Forget relaxing.

I sat up and turned to Julian. "He did?"

He smiled knowingly. Yes, he knew my obsession with Ryan. After I'd asked about the man so many times, Julian sat me down and asked exactly what went on between us. He didn't give me hope to think I could have something, even a friendship, with the man. He just listened and then said at the end, "You never know what the future may bring."

"Yeah, he was in the area and saw the light on. It was lucky it was the one night I stayed up."

I wanted to shake Julian to give me all the information in seconds.

"And?" I pushed, throwing my phone to the bed.

He reached up and tugged on a strand of hair. "And I told him you were doing well."

"Julian," I scolded.

Julian shrugged. "He wasn't here long, but I may have mentioned the nightmares. He gave me something that he thought could help if you can't get back to sleep right away."

"What?" I whispered.

He picked up my phone and pressed a few things on there. The next second, music started up.

My breath caught as I drew it in sharply.

I was over crying. I'd cried a billion times. Only a couple of times had there been tears of happiness, and this was one of those moments.

Ryan had suggested music.

Straight away, it conjured up the image of Ryan singing—even though it wasn't his voice or a song he'd played before. A small smile slowly crept onto my lips.

How could I have been so stupid? Of course music would work for me. I could have hit myself for not thinking of it sooner. Though, I was glad I hadn't, because then Ryan wouldn't have been able to suggest it.

"This music is something you like?" Julian asked.

I nodded.

"Country?"

"Yes. Country had always been playing when I was with my dad." I'd also heard an amazing man sing a certain song, which happened to be the moment my feelings had grown for him.

"Where did you use to live before...?"

Reaching out, I took my phone from his hand and smiled down at it. "A long way out of town on a lot of acres. My dad was a farmer, but he also owned a couple of food stores, along with stocks and shares." I glanced up. "He didn't run them. His life was on the land."

"You miss him," he said.

I knew it wasn't a question, and yet I wanted to answer. "Yes. Every day."

I didn't know my mum, so I couldn't say I missed her. But my dad I would always miss. Just like someone else I knew.

My eyes caught my arm. I only wore a tank top to bed—it was how I was most comfortable—so I could clearly see my defacements. My marks didn't bother Julian and Mattie. I knew that because they encouraged me to wear tees on the hotter days and not the same hoodie I had when Julian stole it out of Ryan's wardrobe.

It took me some time, but I eventually did. They didn't see the scars; they saw me. At least that was what Julian had told me. He also mentioned that whoever I ended up with would see that as well.

It was hard to listen to because when I saw the disfigurements, all I saw was me being ugly, dirty, and weak.

"Did he say anything else?" I whispered into the room. I ran my thumb over the face of my phone as the lyrics sang out.

"They might have a lead on fuckface."

I nodded. It was good to hear, but it would have been better coming from Ryan himself. *Ha, like that'll happen.* A small dose of sadness rolled through me. I pushed it to the back of my mind and said, "I think I might get some more sleep."

"Okay, my dove." He kissed my temple and stood. "I better get some beauty sleep." He winked and started for the door. He turned back at the threshold. "Night, honey."

"Night, Julian." I smiled.

I slid back down, put my phone next to me, and tucked my hands under my cheek. I was a little disappointed that Ryan hadn't come here when he knew I would be awake. I was a little hurt he may have done it because he didn't want to see me. Annoyed for him suggesting the music because it reminded me of him. Yet I was also happy because I knew it would help me sleep. Closing my eyes, the picture wasn't far from my mind—Ryan on the deck singing the song to me. Only that time, I would be sitting on the porch with him.

CHAPTER EIGHTEEN

WARDEN

I was at the front door, about to leave, when a scream filled the house. I started forward, but Julian's palm hit my chest.

"Don't," Julian warned, a tone I'd never heard from him.

Mattie stood behind him, arms crossed over his chest. "Julian, you go to her."

With a final look at me, Julian turned and walked off. He headed for the hallway where I knew Emmie was waking from a nightmare.

I wanted to beat the shit out of myself.

I hated knowing she suffered every damn night because of those motherfuckers.

I hated knowing I couldn't help.

Knowing I didn't fight for her to stay at my place.

Knowing I was attracted to her.

Knowing I cared.

For a woman I didn't really know.

How in the Christ did that happen? It was like she crawled under my skin and stayed there.

The scream had been cut off. I could hear Julian's voice and her soft one replying.

"Warden," Mattie called.

I stopped, hadn't even realised I'd started for the hallway. Clenching my fists, I faced Mattie. "She okay?"

He smiled sadly. "She will be. I think what you suggested before, with the music, will help her get back to sleep quicker."

I'd purposely called in late to see how things were going for Emmie, hoping she'd be in bed. I was a coward. A goddamn coward over a woman because she'd been through hell and I was attracted to her from one fucking glance. Not only that, but she was younger. Way too damn young.

That was why I had to steer clear.

She had her whole life ahead of her.

One where she'd come through from the shitstorm she'd been dealt and grow stronger. Into a beautiful woman. She'd marry, have kids, smile, love, and laugh. She deserved it all.

Yet hearing her scream, I found it bloody hard not to go in there and comfort her.

Fuck. I wanted to take Emmie into my arms and hold her.

This shit was messed up.

I had to keep myself busy, so I didn't weaken and visit like I had again. I needed to stay the hell away, let her be. Thank fuck cases were coming in, and there was still the hunt for Phillip goddamn Burrows. Couldn't believe he'd taken off. Disappeared without a trace.

I was determined to find the dickhead.

Determined to make sure Emmie could breathe without fear consuming her. They'd told me she hadn't even been outside yet. Julian did all the shopping for her after she'd got her bank card back from the house, within her aunt's purse. She'd freaked when the women had visited too. The only people she seemed to like and could be herself around were

Julian, Mattie, and Killer. He was the last man I expected her to feel comfortable around, but she did. From what I heard, if he wasn't patrolling, he visited Emmie a lot. They hardly talked, but they liked to watch some show together.

I hated it.

"Got to go," I told Mattie, heading for the front door again.

"Why don't you call in when she's awake?"

I paused with my hand on the door handle. "It's easier this way."

"For her or you?"

I snorted. It was for me, but for her too.

"Warden," Julian called.

I shifted to meet his gaze and also saw he had the door to the hallway closed. "Never have I seen her smile like that until I played her the music. She knows it came from your suggestion. She appreciates it."

I nodded.

"She cares for you," he added.

I shook my head and smirked. "She's young, doesn't know how to feel or act after goin' through what she did."

Julian glared. "She's smart and so much older in her mind than you give her credit for."

I narrowed my own eyes. "Why the fuck you sayin' this shit for anyway?"

"Because I know you care for her."

I laughed without a trace of humour. "We don't know each other."

"Then get to know one another. Stop running from her."

"This is fuckin' ridiculous," I clipped. "I'm outta here." Before he could say anything else, I turned back to the door and headed outside, closing the door behind me. What I wanted to do was slam the fucker. Knowing she'd be lying down listening to the music I suggested was the only thing that held me back.

Why in the hell did Julian tell me that? *"She cares for you."*

She could. Maybe she did. But it wouldn't be the right way. She could see me as... Christ, maybe her knight in shining armour. Someone who got her out of a hellhole into freedom.

I didn't goddamn know.

"Warden." I looked over my shoulder just as I reached my ute to see Mattie coming my way. "Emmie is—"

"Mattie, just don't."

"I have to."

My phone rang. I held up a finger to Mattie and looked at the screen to see Talon's number. "Gotta take this," I told Mattie, who frowned. "Yeah?"

"Blue caught movement a block away, four guys dressed in black. They're coming in fast. Get back inside."

I ended the call, grabbed Mattie's upper arm, and, on the walk to the house, I said, "Could be some threats coming in fast. Get in the house. Go to Emmie's room with Julian and stay there until one of us comes to get you."

I was surprised when I didn't see Mattie pale in fear. His jaw clenched as he nodded and opened the door.

"Poppet?" Julian asked, standing from the couch.

"Emmie's room, now," Mattie said. "Grab the bat and my gun."

I stepped in and shut the door, locking it. I pulled my gun free from its holster as I turned off the living room light and peeked out from behind the curtain. "Get the light in the kitchen, Mattie."

He did and came back in when Julian reached the living room. Julian handed Mattie his gun. Something Talon would have gotten him because it didn't look legal. Mattie took hold of Julian's hand and led him down the hall.

As I glanced out from behind the curtain again, I heard Emerson's startled cry before one of them reassured her. Someone came up the front walk, a flash of light passing over a vest. Killer.

I unlocked and opened the door quickly.

"Get her in the living room. We'll surround her. Burrows is with the group."

"Fuck." I advanced down the hall and opened the door to Emmie's room. Music played softly as Julian sat on the bed with her while Mattie stood by the window, keeping an eye out.

"Everyone in the living room," I said. I let my gaze drift back over Emmie. She looked pale, and her body trembled a little. She wore only a tank top, and when Julian flicked back the blanket, I caught pink panties. *Damn.* I quickly turned and went back down the hall.

It wasn't the time for pink panties to be burned into my mind.

I also had to wipe away the image of the scars I saw. It wasn't that they made her look bad. She never could. It was the thought of how she got them, what she went through, that had anger rising, along with the fury already burning over the fucker Burrows disturbing what could have been a peaceful rest for Emmie.

I stood by the hallway door. Julian came through first, then Emmie in—*fuck me*—my hoodie and track pants, followed by Mattie.

"On the couch," Killer ordered from where he stood near the front door. "Blue's at the back. Griz has Emmie's bedroom window, Talon the other. We should be covered."

"It's going to be okay, dovey dove," Julian told Emmie, pulling her down to the couch. I moved off to the kitchen and stood in there, looking out the back window into the dark night.

I glanced back to the living room to find Mattie standing over Julian and Emmie. Emmie had her feet up, her arms curled around them as Julian wrapped his arms around her. He whispered in her ear. She nodded. Then her eyes came to me.

I quickly turned back to the window and saw a shadow move across the way.

A shot was fired outside. I ran to the back door and pulled it open. As I stepped out, I heard Emmie's cry of "Ryan." I wanted to look at her, but I had to steel myself and have my head in the situation.

Blue had a guy on the grass who bled from the leg. A gun lay on the garden not far from where they were.

One guy. Three to go.

"Behind," Blue called.

I spun, gun raised, then ducked when a guy fired. I heard glass splintering inside. Adrenaline rushed through me. I tackled the guy to the ground, hit him twice. The crunch of my fist slamming into his flesh sounded good, but I couldn't take pleasure in it, not while Burrows was still at large and Emmie was at risk. There was also the fact that the motherfucker was knocked out cold. Back on my feet, I ran back inside. Killer towered over a guy passed out on the ground. Out the corner of my eye, I saw a flash in the hallway.

"Down," I yelled. Julian covered Emmie's body. Mattie dove over them. I fired as soon as I saw a hand come into view. The dickhead screamed. His weapon dropped. Immediately, I stalked over, kicking it away. Nabbing the piece of crap by the jacket, I pulled him into view. A light in the living room got switched on, and I threw Burrows to the ground, gun aimed down on him.

It couldn't be this easy. He couldn't be this stupid.

"Why now?" I asked. "Why the fuck come here now?"

"Gloria threatened if I didn't kill the bitch, she'd tell the cops where she'd transferred the money we got from our operation."

I shook my head. "Did you seriously think you had a chance at gettin' her?"

"Yes. They promised me they were good at getting in and out."

"The other guys? That're all taken down?"

He ground his teeth. "Yes," he hissed.

I heard the front door open. Lan stepped in. "See I'm late."

"Two out the back," I told him.

"Got it. Others should be here soon." He glanced at Killer. "You and the brothers all covered with the right weapons?"

"Vi's on her way with Butch. They should get here before your crew. She'll have us covered and we'll disappear."

"Good."

"What the fuck is this?" Burrows demanded. "You're a cop. You can't be working with them. I'll tell. I'll—"

Talon stepped up beside me. It was damn lucky I didn't jump or I doubted I'd live it down with them. Talon crouched next to Burrows. "You might want to keep your mouth shut, Burrows. You know who we are?"

He glared up at Talon but said nothing. Talon shifted his foot over Burrows's bleeding hand. He applied pressure, and Burrows yelled, "Stop, stop. Hawks Motorcycle Club."

"You heard about us?" Talon removed his foot.

Burrows whimpered. "Yes," he hissed.

"Then you know we've got people everywhere. If we hear you breathed a word to anyone, we'll go after your mistress, your wife, your kids, and your money that you had hidden in an account overseas. Do you understand?"

He nodded.

"Want words, motherfucker."

"Yes. I get it."

"Good." Talon stood. "Julian, Mattie, and Emmie, you're all in the compound tonight. Pack a bag."

I noticed then that they were already standing. Julian was in front of Emmie, and she had her head buried into his back, gripping his tee. Mattie stood behind her. When Julian shuffled forward, Emmie followed, and their line went straight for the hallway.

Just as they went by me, Emmie turned her head my way. Her gaze ran over me quickly. She caught my eyes, and I nodded. Her eyes welled, but she gave me a small, timid smile before disappearing down the hall.

My job was done.

She was free.

Burrows would go to jail, and Emmie could breathe easy.

I didn't have to see her again.

Christ, that thought stabbed my chest.

CHAPTER NINETEEN

EMERSON

*K*iller was alone in the living room when we walked back out with our overnight bags. My shoulders slumped. I had hoped Ryan would still be there, but he'd done it again. Disappeared.

I couldn't believe the night.

The fear I'd felt.

It wasn't because Phillip Burrows had been there either. I knew the people around me had the matter at hand. I'd come to trust and realise they were true to their words. Instead, fear claimed me for the men involved. Especially when Ryan ran out the back door into the fray.

It was crazy as I knew he was competent in his job. I'd heard some stories from Julian and Mattie about the women with the Hawks men. A lot of the stories were mind-blowing and super scary. Some of what the women had been through was even worse than what I'd experienced. However, all of them had come out well in the end. And that was because of the Hawks men, as well as Ryan and his work colleagues.

Killer opened the front door and walked out first. Julian

pushed me ahead so I could follow Killer. Then Julian was behind me with Mattie.

We crossed the road to the compound. The place was lit up. There were vehicles everywhere. When Killer opened the door, I didn't want to step through. Tension shivered down my spine. How many people would be in there?

"You're good here," Killer said.

I nodded. "I know." And I did, because the men in the club were amazing. I knew it from experience and how Julian gloated about them.

We went through the door, down a hallway, and then into a large open space where there were couches, seats, a pool table, some arcade games, and a bar. There were also a few men and women around. Two women, in fact, and when they saw us, they approached slowly. I shifted behind Killer. Julian and Mattie came to my side, but it was Julian who put his arm around my waist.

"Hey, honey," one of the women said.

"Cupcake." Wait, what? Cupcake? Had that really come out of Killer's mouth? I knew he had an "old lady"—not that I really understood what that was—but I'd never seen her before. Or his reaction to her. Killer's voice was in a tone I hadn't heard. Sweet, soft, and loving. He leaned forward, cupping the woman's jaw, and kissed her as if no one was around to see it. I witnessed her melt into him, her arms sliding around his waist. At the end of the kiss, he curled his arm around her shoulders and turned to face me. It was then that the other woman stepped up to Mattie and hugged his waist, which he replicated.

"Em, this is my old lady, Ivy. Ivy, meet Emmie."

"Hi, Emmie. I've heard so much about you. All good, I promise. I'm sorry for what you went through. It's disgusting what some people do. Family can totally suck sometimes. But it's good that you're healing. Julian and Mattie are the perfect people to be around when that happens because they're kind, funny, and sweet. I just bet—"

"Babe," Killer said.

Ivy blushed. "Sorry. My mouth gets the better of me sometimes."

My lips twitched. She was… adorable. The tightness in my chest eased.

"It's nice to meet you, Ivy."

Her smile was bright. "You too."

"Emmie," Mattie called. I looked to him and the woman at his side; they looked similar. "This is my sister, Zara. Zara, Emmie."

"Hey, it's great to see you, Emmie. I'm sorry about what just happened. Though I'm sure the guys had it all in hand."

I nodded. "They did." If I remembered correctly, Zara was married to Talon, and they had four children together.

"We've set up a room for you. A lot of the brothers sleep elsewhere, so it was easy to get two rooms close together."

Two rooms?

Wait, I'd be staying on my own?

At a compound full of bikers?

Yes, I trusted them; they'd proven I could, but it was still daunting after what just happened. People broke into Julian and Mattie's place to kill me. Because my aunt wanted me dead.

Could there be more people after me?

Would she send more?

Was I actually free?

I glanced at Killer. "Will she send more?"

I didn't need to elaborate. He understood because he replied with "No. We've kept an eye on her. Burrows was the only one she communicated with besides her lawyer. He's one of ours, even though he's supposed to work for her. She won't get out and she won't contact anyone we don't know about. We've got people on the inside to make sure we can watch her there as well."

"You're really safe now, my dove," Julian said, giving my waist a squeeze.

I lifted my gaze to his. "I am," I whispered, then smiled.

But would being safe give me the strength to go out in the world without a care?

Maybe in time, yes.

It always came down to time. At least now I knew I had more time on my hands than I thought I ever would. There would be no more thinking of dying.

I was free.

"Woman" was called.

Before I could see who it was, I caught Zara grumbling under her breath. Then, with a tight smile firm on her lips, she turned. Mattie's arms dropped away.

"Here they go," Ivy sang low.

My brows dipped in confusion until Zara planted her hands on her hips and glared at Talon. "Don't you 'woman' me, Talon Marcus. You do not run out of here holding a gun, saying there's a situation, and scare the heck out of me."

He rolled his eyes. "Woman, there was a situation."

"I know that, Talon, but every time you go out guns ablazing, do you think you could take a second to kiss me and tell me you love me? The last thing I said to you was that you were a jerk and weren't getting any tonight. Do you think I want to remember that's the last thing you'll think about if something happens?"

His smirk was cocky. "Kitten, I had it in hand. You had nothin' to worry about. Plus, I know you were talkin' shit. I so am gettin' some tonight and you know it."

She threw her hands up in the air. "That's beside the point."

Were they really talking about sex in front of everyone? I glanced around. A lot of the group seemed amused by the scene, but I got the feeling this wasn't out of the ordinary. No one was as shocked as I was with my wide eyes and gaping mouth.

He got close to her, slid an arm around her, and dragged her into him. When he whispered something in her ear, she nodded but smacked his chest. I heard him chuckle and then murmur something else. Then she kissed him.

Julian's finger tapped my chin. I snapped my mouth closed and he laughed. "It's all right. They argue all the time, but the chemistry they have together makes up for it."

Not sure what to say, I nodded.

I wanted that.

Wanted what Zara had with Talon.

What Killer had with Ivy, and Julian with Mattie.

I wanted someone to care about and love with fierceness.

Of course I thought of Ryan, but I pushed his image away quickly before it could take hold and let my surprisingly good mood, considering everything that had happened, fade.

Ivy caught my gaze. "How about I show you the rooms? I'm sure you're tired after everything. I know I would be. I mean"—she rolled her eyes—"I know I'm here late, but it was a night out with my man, and we like those nights late. Thank God I have people who work for me or else I'll be dead on my feet tomorrow. And since Zara was here earlier, she decided to hang, especially when Nancy and Richard, her parents, offered to have the kids for the night."

"Babe," Killer said, though he did it smiling.

"Right." She clapped. "Rooms. Let's go." We left Talon and Zara behind and made our way down another hall. I got a few looks from some of the men around. None of them made my skin crawl like Lenny's used to. I felt reassured by it.

Trust.

It was time to show them I could trust, that I could be brave, even after what just happened.

We stopped at a door, which Ivy opened. "For Mattie and Julian."

"Actually, Mattie will stay in here. I'll be with Emmie," Julian told her. She looked to me, and already I was shaking my head.

"No. You stay with your man."

"Dove—"

I rested my hands on his chest. "I know after what just happened, you would think I'd be in a state. You would think staying in someplace new would add to it also, but I'm not. I can't say I won't wake you having nightmares, but that's normal for us." I smiled, as did Julian. "I know I'm safe. I know I'm free, and I know I can trust these people around me. Let me show that, at least, by being able to stay in a room on my own in a place I don't know."

His hand covered mine. He leaned in and kissed my temple. "Okay, my brave dove."

"Thank you," I whispered. Mattie came forward, gave me a hug, and they both walked into the bedroom, closing the door behind them. I looked down the hall where we'd come from and my body tingled in apprehension. I forced it to stop. I faced Ivy and Killer.

"My room's there?" I pointed to the one behind them, next to Julian and Mattie's.

Ivy nodded. Slowly, she reached out and took my hand in hers. She guided me to the door and opened it. "It's not the best place to stay. Not like the Sheraton or anything. But seriously, I can't see bikers wanting to stay at a place like that; it'd be too toffy for them." She laughed. "At least this place is clean, warm, and more welcoming than a hotel. All the doors have locks, and this room has its own en suite. I gave it to you and not the guys because us women need a bathroom close. Though, Julian probably looks at himself more than we would." She waved her hands around. "I'm not being mean or anything. I'm just saying he's good-looking. He makes sure of it with all his routines. You know what I mean, right?"

Her bumbling words reminded me of how comfortable I felt with Julian right away. Ivy was the same. The way she was could put a smile on anyone's face. To put her at ease, I said, "I know what you mean. I've seen all his routines; it's no wonder his skin is perfect."

"Exactly." She smiled and we both laughed. I tensed when she hugged me next. If she felt it, she didn't react, but she pulled back and said, "I hope you get some much-needed rest."

"Thank you." I glanced at Killer. "Thanks again for—"

He grabbed the back of Ivy's neck and gently ushered her into walking. "Don't mention it."

Smiling, I waved at Ivy before Killer shut the door. I went over to lock it and then spun back around, leaning against it. Even though my heart had crawled up into my throat at the thought of being alone in there, I still moved away from the door and got into the fresh-smelling bed.

I could do this.

It was the start of my new beginning, because I was finally and completely free.

CHAPTER TWENTY

EMERSON

*E*ven though all of the people from my nightmares had been behind bars for six months and I knew I was safe, I still woke some nights screaming and sweating. It might've had something to do with living on my own now. The quietness to the house. There wasn't a Julian coming in to wake me. No Mattie to brush my hair at night when we watched *Santa Clarita's Diet*.

At least they weren't far. We could still do those things. I could still see them every day if I wanted to, since they were right next door. With Dad's life insurance, I'd purchased Talon's property that he never really used but kept because he didn't want anyone in the house.

It was amazing to know I had them right next door, but it was the waking late at night that I didn't like doing on my own. The music helped, a lot, and I knew one day the dreams would end. I just hoped it would be soon. However, it didn't look like it.

I rolled over in bed. My room was lit by another night light. This one was a moving-in gift from Julian. It wasn't one that plugged straight into the power point. It was on a cord that sat on my bedside table. It was of a moon sitting on clouds. While it seemed childish, I loved it.

I loved all of the things in my room and house. It was only a small, one-bedroom unit, but it was mine. I'd paid for it fair and square. And having a place I could call my own, that was safe, was worth the quietness.

Things were slowly coming together in my life. I had a job. In fact, it was my own business designing logos. I started doing courses online, everything I could learn to make sure I'd get my bachelor's degree in graphic design. Photoshop was tricky to get around at the start, since I was used to drawing, but I was getting there. Somehow, while studying, I still managed to gain a few clients as I worked on my degree. Thankfully, those clients were happy with what I produced on paper and not computer and promised to spread the word about my work. I also mentioned to them that I would soon be up to date with some desktop design software, including that darn Photoshop. The best part about it all was how I got to work from home, doing whatever hours I wanted, at my little setup in the corner of my living room.

I'd gained weight, though I was sure most of it went to my butt and stomach, but I didn't mind. I was happy with how I looked…. Sort of, at least. I never went out of the house, even on the hot days, without a long-sleeved top and something to cover my legs. I didn't want people to see my scars. That was an insecurity I wouldn't get over fast.

I'd been out of the house more than I wanted, mainly because of Julian or Ivy dragging me to places.

The first time I went in public, Julian took me to Donny's grave. I sat there crying the whole time and apologising while Julian held me. Guilt was still raw over what happened to him.

I didn't think I would ever stop blaming myself; it was something I'd have to learn to live with. Eventually.

The second time we went out was for a celebratory dinner with Julian, Mattie, Ivy, Killer, Zara, Talon, Violet—who still scared me a little because she was a little on the feisty side— her husband, Travis, and Butch. No Ryan. He'd been busy apparently. They hired out a private room at a restaurant to celebrate the incarceration of the people who'd tried to destroy my life. Gloria, Lenny, Jarrod, and Phillip Burrows had been sentenced to forty years behind bars. They wouldn't be up for parole for two decades, and by then, they'd either be dead or would be too old to even think of revenge. At least I hoped.

What was better had been the lead-up to the court case. I hadn't had to face them. My drawings, book, and interview had been enough so I didn't have to make an appearance in the court. Plus they had so much footage of the young women who they'd harmed as hard evidence. My name and face had been all over the TV. Reporters wanted to interview me, but to my surprise, and relief, Violet took care of everything—her number was listed as my contact. Talon had also suggested keeping my name off the house title for now, until things died down and my case was old news. I couldn't agree more, so he'd be keeping his name on there until people forgot about me.

The day after our celebratory dinner, Julian took me to the hairdresser, where they trimmed and layered my long dark hair. When I'd seen the finished cut in the mirror, I'd gasped and slowly reached up to touch my soft locks. It made me feel beautiful, and for the rest of the day, I moved with a new spring in my step. Other times I ventured out, my new friends took me to the bookstore or to Ivy's café, and a couple of times we went to the movies. Though the movies I didn't like so much due to it always being busy. I hadn't yet been to any shopping centres, fearing the large crowds. I wasn't sure why crowds made me lose my breath, but they did.

Heck, I'd even been on a date. It was with a regular customer of Ivy's. He was a tradesman, but she assured me he was sweet. He had been. We got along well enough, made small talk over dinner as we sat in a diner, one Ivy knew wasn't busy.

By the end of it though, we'd both known it wouldn't work. He'd dropped me back to Ivy's café, where she'd been waiting for me since I refused to be picked up from home. I hadn't wanted him to know where I lived. When he'd left Ivy's café, we'd hugged. He hadn't even gone in for a kiss. While we'd enjoyed each other's time together, he wasn't....

He wasn't the one I wanted to be out with.

The one I wanted to talk with.

The one I dreamed of.

He wasn't the man who constantly played on my mind.

It annoyed and angered me.

Why wasn't I good enough for Ryan?

Was it my age? My personality? Then again, he had never taken the time to get to know the real me. Could it be my looks? My scars?

I didn't know, and I'd been wondering a lot lately if I should try and reach out myself.

If I texted, would he answer?

If I rang—though even the thought made me break out in a sweat—would he answer?

Reaching out, I stroked a finger over my phone.

I picked it up and rolled to my back, lighting up the screen. First, I went to Spotify—the app Julian had installed for the music—and pressed on my folder for country music. It started with a song about breaking hearts, and even though it was sad, I smiled. I grinned because it was country music and it always reminded me of Ryan.

I licked my dry lips and went into my messages.

My stomach and heart felt one and the same, like they both wanted out of my body before I did what I was about to do.

I pulled the covers up more. Even on the warm nights, my body chilled with nerves.

Once I read over the questions he'd sent me so many months ago, it was finally time to answer them. Then the ball would be in his court. If he messaged back, I would know he wanted something from me. Even if it was friendship, I wouldn't complain because Ryan would be in my life. My heart may hurt for a while, but I would make myself get over it.

I've never had nachos, but my favourite food right now would be... pizza. Who doesn't love a good slice of barbeque meatlovers? Having gone without pizza for such a long time, when I'd tried it again with Julian and Mattie, I decided there and then that I would eat it every day for the rest of my life. If I could get away with it. Along with chocolate, of course.

To answer about reading, yes, I love it. I read over watching TV all the time.

Of course you had to ask if I liked sports. The answer is I've never really watched any. I might like football, as you do, but I haven't figured that out yet. I wished I had the strength to add that I'd find out with him when he watched it, but I didn't.

When you asked: Is Emmie short for something? And you provided your guesses, I laughed at each one of them. Especially Emmit. At least you know what it's short for now. I still found myself laughing over his suggestions.

Has Butch stolen any more lunches from you? Have you hit him yet for it?

You questioned: Are you okay? I can finally say, yes, I am okay. And it had a lot to do with his help.

Do you like Disney? I've never really seen a Disney

movie. **Before my dad died, I spent my days on the farm, mainly feeding the animals, cleaning up after them, mowing, cleaning, and sometimes cooking if I wanted to eat something without wanting to throw up. Dad's cooking had been hit and miss. It was miss a lot of the times. Still, he was the best Dad there was.**

When you wrote: Some days I hate my job when I can't find the answers I want. My heart went out to you. I didn't know at the time what you did for a living. Now I understand it more, and I hope with whatever you're working on you find the answers fast.

It took me five goes to press Send. Immediately, I regretted it, having forgotten it was so late. I hoped I hadn't woken him; that would be annoying.

When I didn't receive anything back half an hour later, I forced myself to put my phone down and roll away from it. Eyes wide open, I stared at the wall, my brain working overtime. Had I made the right choice in texting him?

Had I come across too strong? Could he tell I liked him from my answers? Did he think I was just a naïve young girl hero-worshipping him?

What would happen if I mentioned that time I saw him with the woman? How it made me feel, how I wished it was me who he was with?

No, that would definitely be embarrassing, creepy, and could make me sound like a foolish little girl.

Even when I wished Ryan would be my first.

Which was crazy, because I hardly knew him, and yet I still felt like I did.

Maybe it was because of all of the time I'd spent watching him without him noticing me. Though, honestly, I couldn't deny my attraction to the man. Right from the start, even with all the men I'd seen, Ryan had stood out above them all. Was it just attraction leading my heart and mind? I didn't know, but I wanted to find out what or *if* we could be something to each other.

I would have to wait and see if he messaged back, but I refused to stay up all night thinking about it all.

Closing my eyes, I listened to the music and hoped it would take me into slumber.

Eventually it did, but the dream I had didn't help.

It was of Ryan and me out on his back deck. We were drinking, talking, and I braved it enough to approach him sitting on his chair. I straddled his thighs and told him he'd been the only one for me.

He stared up and smiled. His hand slid to the back of my neck and he drew my mouth down towards his, but before our lips touched, I woke with the sun shining through the gaps in the curtain. I rolled to my back and cursed at the ceiling. I thought about going back to sleep, to chase the dream, but I knew it would be useless. Instead, I got up, showered, and started my day. I only looked at my phone every few minutes, but still, by the end of the day, there was no reply. No matter how many times I checked.

CHAPTER TWENTY-ONE

WARDEN

*W*hat in the fuck was I doing there? Just because Julian had mentioned Emmie had a set routine, which included one day a week when she visited Ivy's coffee shop as she worked on her laptop, I was there like a stalker. She'd messaged me just a few days ago, answering the questions I'd sent at the start. When she'd been held in the basement.

I wanted to reply. Fuck, I really wanted to, but I didn't.

I couldn't lead her on, even if it was just friendship she wanted from me. I couldn't give that to her, not when I wanted more. And she was too damn young. I had to remind myself of the fact over and over.

Shit, I was getting sick of myself saying it.

When I'd heard Ivy talking to Mally at the compound one night about how proud she was of Emmie going on her first date, I'd nearly crushed the beer bottle in my hand. Instead of listening to more, I got up and left.

It'd put a foul taste in my mouth. Thinking of Emmie out

on a date with some young dickhead. Fuck, just thinking of her on a date with anyone cut at my gut.

Christ, I wanted her.

I goddamn did.

There, I admitted it to myself.

I wanted Emerson Spence for myself. So much so that I hadn't even looked at a woman since the day she'd walked out from the basement.

Did I man the fuck up and go over there, talk to her, get to know her, or keep hiding in my corner and watching her like the fucking freak I was as she chewed on a pencil while typing something on her laptop?

She hadn't noticed me when she walked in, which I was grateful for. But if Ivy got back from wherever she was, she'd see me, call me out, and then Emmie would know I was there. Stalking her.

Fuck me. I was a sorry son-of-a-bitch.

She looked good. In fact, since I hadn't seen her in so long, I almost didn't recognise her when she came in. Her hair was longer, styled just nice. Her body had filled out in all the right ways, and she radiated happiness.

Was she still having nightmares?

Did she still wake from them and then listen to the music I suggested?

Was she scared in the house on her own?

When Talon told me he was selling his house next to Zara's old one, the one where Julian and Mattie lived, I was surprised. He only owned it because he didn't want a stranger to buy it across the road from the compound. Of course, I asked who he'd sold it to, and when he said it was Emmie, I didn't like it.

Not that she couldn't have her own place. Hell, I was happy she wanted her independence.

I didn't like the thought of her being alone at night as that was when her nightmares plagued her.

At least when she was with Julian and Mattie, they could go to her if they heard her.

Now she was all alone.

What was it about Emerson Spence that brought out my instinct to want to protect her more than anyone else? To want her more than any other woman?

She'd made a rare connection within me and it wouldn't be removed.

Couldn't.

I thought it'd end when the case did.

It hadn't.

She was still on my mind.

And from her texts to me, I was on hers too. I just didn't know if it was in more than a friendship way. Yeah, Julian had said she cared, but in what way?

Christ, was I just an old man pining over a younger woman when all she wanted was a friend in me?

Could I give that to her when I wanted more?

Fucked if I knew.

My head was a goddamn mess when it came to her.

Maybe if I got to know her more, I'd figure out she wasn't for me after all. Nodding to myself, I got up, went to the counter, paid my bill, and walked out.

It was time to figure out how I really felt about Emmie.

Time to get to know her... only it wouldn't be in person. It'd have to be over the phone, because I was sure as fuck physically attracted to her. But would her personality work for me as well?

EMERSON

I sat on the couch watching *Lucifer* on Netflix and eating cheese and bacon balls when my phone vibrated. I was expecting Julian and Mattie over shortly, since Julian offered to make some pasta dish for dinner later, so I thought it would be either one of them.

It wasn't.

My breath shot out in a whoosh as my eyes widened. Slowly, in case it was my eyes playing tricks on me, I picked up my phone from the couch beside me and looked closely.

It still read the same.

I had stored his number a long time ago, so to see his name on my screen for the first time in so long was a complete shock. One that had my body in a tizzy.

If I opened it, would I like what I saw? If he was brushing me off, at least I knew where we stood, and I'd deal with it over a tub of Ben and Jerry's. Maybe it would be more than one.

Though, waiting wasn't doing my heart any good.

I pressed in the code to unlock my phone, and then I went right into messages. I needed to get it out of the way as soon as possible. If it was bad, and Julian and Mattie arrived to see me crying, I wasn't sure they wouldn't pay Ryan a visit.

Ryan: Meatlovers is good, but I prefer barbeque chicken, Emmie. He was answering my texts from a couple of nights ago. He was acting normal. Like we'd been texting each other all the time. Then again, I had done the same, but I was reaching out to him to see if he wanted to engage back.

He had.

He messaged me back.

He wanted to talk.

To get to know one another.

But I couldn't jump to conclusions yet. I'd wait and see

where this went… but I was darn excited to be in contact with him. So excited that I let out a little squeal and kicked my feet up and down. Cheese and bacon balls went flying, but I didn't care. Instead, I read on.

If you haven't tried it, you should. I won't hate on you for reading. A lot of the women I know do it. Football is life. You should see if you like it. Butch is still being a dick. He's taken a couple more meals from me. But I did it back to him today and the douche didn't like it at all. Maybe he'll stop now. Glad to hear you're doing well, darlin'. Now every-thing's over, even the court case and all, I hope you're breathing easy. Was surprised you haven't seen Disney movies. Even more surprised to learn you worked on a farm. Your dad sounds like a good guy. Glad you had him in your life. Sucks it ended so early for you. The cases I have right now are doing my head in. But nothing too bad, which is good.

Heard you've got your own place and set up your own business. That's bloody great, Emmie. What else have you been up to?

He'd heard things about me. From who? Had he asked or just been told?

At least he was asking about me now. That meant some-thing, right?

If I texted back right away, did it show I was too eager? Desperate for his attention?

Screw it all. I wasn't one to play mind games. He could take me replying straight away any way he wanted to.

Emmie: I'll be sure to give that pizza a try, maybe one time when I'm also figuring out football. I hope Butch doesn't try again. Then again if he does, you should set him up and have something hidden in your lunch that will make him never steal your food again.

I'll never say I won't try Disney movies.... I heard Julian talk about them the other day, and I have a feeling if he found out I've never seen one, it would change, and quickly. I loved working on the farm. I miss it a lot. And yes, you're right, Dad was an amazing man.

Sorry to hear your cases are playing on your mind, but at least, like you've said, it's not too bad.

I do have my own place and business. I live right next door to Julian and Mattie. It's small, but perfect for just me. I took a couple of online courses to develop my graphic design skills and get into branding, things like designing logos. As it happens, I have a natural talent for it, so I've been told. The clients I have were willing to hire me even though I hadn't finished the courses. From them being happy with my work, they've spread the word, and I've managed to gain a couple more clients. It's small right now, which suits me just fine, but I am hoping to grow it eventually. Say in a few years.

Honestly, my days have been filled with work, courses, and taking back my life. Making my days how I want them. You might know already, but there was enough money in Dad's accounts for me to live comfortable until my inheritance comes in. I could sit around and do nothing if I really wanted to, but for me, that's not life.

Life is about making your own mark. My dad had his with his businesses and the farm. I want to make my own. I'm not even sure why I'm telling you that.

Anyway. I have some questions for you.

Do you eat chocolate? My favourite is Nestle Smarties. But in the block size.

What do you do in your time off?

How do you like your steak cooked? I'm a medium-well to well-done kind of lady.

Do you watch TV? Julian and Mattie have me hooked on a few shows on Netflix. So much so I had to make sure I had Netflix at my own house.

I quickly hit Send before I chickened out, then put the phone back on the couch. It didn't stop me from staring at it, but at least I wasn't holding it.

I heard footsteps on the front porch, and when a key was inserted in the lock, I didn't bother getting up to check who it was. Only two people had keys to my place, so I knew it was either one of them or both Julian and Mattie.

The door swung open. I peeled my eyes from my phone and rubbed at my chest while I looked up at Julian and Mattie in the doorway.

"What happened?" Mattie asked.

I glanced around me, completely forgetting about the cheese and bacon balls everywhere.

"I got a text."

"And that caused you to throw chips about?" Julian asked with an open-mouthed smile. Mattie moved off into the kitchen with the bags he carried. I heard him dump them on the counter and then come back into the room.

He leaned over the back of the couch. "Hey, honey," he said before kissing my temple.

"Hey, honey, back."

"No, seriously, before you get some lovin' off me, who texted?" Julian asked. His hands went to his hips.

"Ryan," I told them.

Julian's eyes widened comically. His hands slid up to cover his mouth. He spread his fingers and whispered, "Warden?"

I nodded. "Ryan Warden."

"What did he want?" Mattie asked, the steady, calm one in our group.

I picked up my phone and waved it about. "Just random

things really. He got back to texts I responded to a couple of days ago, and then he just asked about the house and work."

"He texted," Julian cried.

My smile was jaw aching. "He did."

"Did you reply?"

"I did."

"And?"

"Nothing yet, but that was just before you guys walked through the door." Then my phone vibrated.

"OMG!" Julian screamed. He came at me, grabbed my wrist, and pulled me up to stand. "Go, bedroom. See what he says, answer him, and then tell us if we need to reschedule due to your texting date."

"Julian," Mattie warned.

I gave him a reassuring smile. "Don't worry. I promise I won't get ahead of all this. I won't turn my feelings into more just because he's finally talking and paying attention to me. So far it seems like a friendship, and I'm good with that."

I was, and I would be… I was pretty sure.

As I walked from the bedroom after reading Ryan's replies and then answering his new questions, I stood in the doorway of the kitchen when my phone vibrated again. I glanced down. It was Ryan, again.

"Is that him, after you've just replied?" Julian asked.

"Yes." I nodded and bit my bottom lip so I didn't beam my smile at them.

"We've made a quick grilled chicken and salad for you. But we'll catch up soon for dinner. For now, you enjoy your night texting Warden."

"You don't have to leave."

"Dove, if that was the man who'd been on my mind for over half a year, then I would want time alone to bask in the new friendship. Though, I think—"

"Julian," Mattie clipped.

Julian's lips snapped together. He glared over at his man, then sighed. "Sorry, I won't say what I think because I don't want to get anyone's hopes up. But let me tell you, if that man's just messing with you, I'm going to sneak into his room, cut off—"

"Julian," Mattie bit out.

Julian sighed. "All I was going to say was that I would crush him." Julian stepped up to me with Mattie at his back. "You take care, my dovey dove, but enjoy chatting with Warden."

"You can stay—"

His fingers pressed down on my lips. "Hush now. I'll want to know everything tomorrow."

"Okay," I mumbled around his fingers.

Julian kissed my cheek and walked by, while Mattie stepped up. His smile wasn't fully there. I grabbed his hand and squeezed. "Don't worry about this. I promise I'll be guarded."

"I care. I can't stop it now."

"I know, and I'm so glad I have you and Julian in my life."

"Take care," he whispered against my temple.

"I will."

As soon as they left, I sat at the counter with my dinner in front of me, texting back and forth with Ryan. It was strange since it had been so long, and I wondered why the change in him, but it was also exciting. I hadn't felt giddy like that since the night he sang that song for me.

I would never admit to Mattie that I was worried myself how all this would turn out.

CHAPTER TWENTY-TWO

WARDEN

*W*alking into the compound common room, I found the place busy with brothers and some of their women. I went straight to the bar, hoping a drink would get my mind off texting Emmie. We'd been going back and forth for nearly a month, and doing so made it more dangerous because I was growing to care for the woman even more. With each conversation I had, I learned more and more. What I found out, I liked.

She was smart, funny, sweet, teasing, and just damn charming in all aspects. She knew what she wanted, and after being dealt shit, she still strived for it because she wanted to make her own way in the world.

Not many could do that after what she'd been through. It just proved how bloody strong she was.

Hell, she was right across the road. I could go over there and see her. Like she'd asked me to on a couple of occasions, like that night, but I'd said I couldn't. That I was busy. The real reason was that I knew my resolve would crash and burn. I'd confess I had feelings for her, and I couldn't do that to her. She deserved someone her own age.

She did.

Even though I'd probably kill the guy if he tried to take her out.

Blue stood behind the bar. He saw me approach and grabbed out a beer, holding it up to me. I nodded, and as soon as I got close, I took it, taking a big gulp.

"Rough night?" Blue asked.

"Somethin' like that." I sat on a stool next to Stoke.

He glanced at me after finishing a conversation with Killer and gave me a chin lift. "How's things, Warden?"

"Could be better," I replied. "What's been happenin' around here?" *Please tell me anything to keep my mind busy.*

"Same old. Which is good."

Yeah, it was good for them, having nothing crazy happening, but I could really do with a distraction. Even work had slowed. The only case I was on at the moment was that of a cheating wife.

"Ryan!" was cried. Next, someone crashed into my back and arms circled my neck. "Ryan, Ryan, Ryan. It's good to see you," Mally muttered into my shoulder.

"Jesus," Stoke mumbled. "Woman, get your toasted arse here."

Chuckling, I patted Mally's arm. She let go enough to come to my side. I slid an arm around her waist. "How you doin', darlin'?"

Her smile nearly took over her whole face. "Great. Amazing. I'm so in love with that man right there." She pointed to Stoke. He tried to look annoyed, probably over her being at my side, but he was failing. His lips twitched.

"That's good to know."

She nodded. "It is. He's the bestest of the best."

"You don't say."

"I do," she exclaimed and shook me a little with her arm around my shoulders. Damn, she was a cute drunk. At least I knew she'd be getting home safe. Her man would make sure of it, and it seemed he was nursing some juice drink.

Out the corner of my eye, I caught someone entering the common room. My body locked when I noticed it was Emmie. She nodded and smiled shyly at some of the brothers, then headed over to the couch area. That was when I saw Mattie sitting there talking with Talon.

Mattie looked up at her with a grin. Talon said something, which she replied to. Mattie stood and stopped next to her.

"Ryan," Mally whined, both her arms wrapped around me again. She hugged me close. "My man won't dance with me. You will, right? Please, Ryan. Please."

"Love, I think it's time we head out," Stoke said.

I happened to glance back over at Emmie, hoping Stoke could get control of his woman clinging to me. Her eyes were already on mine, but I didn't like what I saw in them. I watched her look to Mally, her lips thin and her eyes closed, before she nodded to herself. Mattie saw where she'd been looking.

She said something and started for the door. Mattie called after her.

Fuck. Did she think I was there with another woman?

Standing, I gently forced Mally into Stoke's arms and started for the door.

EMERSON

"Emmie, wait. Emmie," Mattie called, and I quickly walked back across the road to his and Julian's place. Julian had sent me over to tell Mattie he was about to miss out on the popcorn and movie. Even though I'd been a bundle of nerves walking in there, I did it. Because I'd gotten to know a lot of them in the previous months. They were all nice men.

When I made it to Mattie, who was speaking with Talon at the couches, Talon asked me how I was doing on the new design for the garage logo. Just after I mentioned it was going well, I heard loud girly laughter and then the woman calling Ryan's name.

I snapped my gaze over to see a woman draped all over Ryan, begging him for a dance.

Ryan was there.

At the compound.

And yet he'd said he'd been too busy to see me. I was getting sick of texting back and forth and wanted to talk with him in person. He wouldn't even answer his phone if I called, made up some bullshit. Just like he had for missing movie night at Julian's house.

What had he said? It was something about being behind on paperwork.

Anger boiled in my stomach, but most of all, hurt scratched at my chest.

Hurt because he had been lying.

Hurt because he'd been there drinking, having fun, and all he had to do was tell me he didn't want to see me. He didn't want to face me. He wanted to have fun with his friends. All of the reasons I would have accepted.

If all he ever wanted was a friendship through texting, then he could have told me.

Maybe he was worried about me being too young and not understanding, but I did.

He obviously knew I wasn't the one for him. I just needed him to say something.

"Emmie," Mattie called again.

I glanced over my shoulder. "I'm fine," I told him. I opened their front door and stomped inside.

"Emmie," Mattie said softly from behind me as I stepped inside the door and curled my arms around my waist.

"I'm fine," I said again.

I heard Mattie close the door and glanced up to see Julian walk into the living room. "What's going on?" he asked.

"Emmie, that wasn't what it looked like with Warden," Mattie said.

I snorted. "It doesn't matter. Really, I'm fine." At least I would be.

I jumped when their door opened with a bang. Mattie and I spun that way. Ryan stood in the doorway, his eyes on me.

"Emerson—"

I waved my hand around. A noise, half snort and half growl, dropped from my lips. "I don't know what you're doing here, Ryan. But it's fine. *Everything* is fine. Go back to the party."

"What's going on?" Julian asked again.

Mattie moved by me and shushed his man.

Ryan stepped into the room and it suddenly felt smaller. He closed the door and took another step my way. I took one back.

"That was my friend Mally. Her man was right there with us."

I laughed without humour. "Why are you telling me this?"

His big-arse feet took another step. I backed up.

"Why do you have tears, darlin'?" he asked softly.

Tears?

I wiped at my face angrily. "I don't know," I snapped. I pulled my sleeves down over my hands and gripped the material. I lifted both arms and held one around my waist, the other over my chest.

He groaned, probably in annoyance for running after a stupid little girl. "I know I said I was busy, but—"

"But you didn't want to come here." My stomach clenched. "That's fine, Ryan. It's fine." My heart beat so hard that it started to ache.

"She's saying fine a lot. That's not good," I heard Julian comment.

"Emmie, that's not—"

"I know." I nodded, more to myself than him. More tears filled my eyes as I glanced down at the floor.

"Know what?" Ryan asked quietly. His voice still grumbled though.

I blinked and tears dropped. "I know you see me as too young. I know I'm not what you want. I know—"

"Baby, don't—"

"I know I'm still mixed up. Why else would I still dream of it? I know... I know I'm never going to be good enough for you—"

"Christ, Emmie. Don't."

But I couldn't stop. I just couldn't. "That's okay, Ryan." I smiled sadly at the floor. "It's okay." I shrugged. "All you had to do was tell me. I know I shouldn't have held out hope for something more between us—"

"Emerson," he growled out, but his voice also held pain.

How was I hurting him?

"But I did, and I understand now that I would never be your type. I'm not... enough. I have scars." My throat caught for a moment. "You deserve someone you want. Someone perfect for you. You really do."

"Baby doll," Ryan tried again, this time on a whisper.

I shook my head and wiped at my tears. My sleeve lifted as I did; I slowly lowered my arm and ran fingers over the marks there. "You don't need anyone broken. Anyone like me."

"Fuckin' hell," he clipped. My eyes snagged on his feet as he stepped close. His big hands cupped my cheeks and he lifted my head so he could have my gaze.

"You don't have to—"

"Shut it, baby doll. It's my turn." His eyes ran over my face. I reached up to take his wrists so I could pull his hands away from my face, but his next words had me stilling. "The only thing holding me back from wanting to see where this could go for us is your age. *You* deserve someone better, someone your own age."

"I only see you," I told the stupid man.

His jaw clenched. His eyes drifted down to my lips. And then he kissed me. It was soft and sweet, but I needed more. I wrapped my arms around his neck and tugged him closer. He made a noise in the back of his throat before deepening the kiss. My mouth opened under his. Immediately, his tongue swept in and played with my own. My body quivered, my heart skipped down to my belly and swirled in a pleasant motion. The kiss was more than I'd ever imagined.

Too soon, he pulled back. "Dinner. Tomorrow night. You and me."

I nodded.

He touched his lips to mine quickly and started for the door. He glanced over his shoulder. "Pick you up at six," he said as he opened the door.

"Okay," I whispered. Distractedly, my fingers pressed against my swollen lips. I caught Ryan's soft smile just for me, and that spread goosebumps over my arms from the excitement that flooded my body.

His gaze ran over me. He nodded and left, closing the door behind him.

"Holy fuck," Julian drew out.

My face heated when I turned to them. To be completely

honest, I'd forgotten they'd been there. Mattie stood close beside Julian, who held Mattie's hand out in front of his chest —no doubt Mattie's hand had been over Julian's mouth.

"Did that really happen?" I asked, unsure if my mind was playing tricks on me. My body still wasn't acting normal, my pulse was up, my hands shook, and I couldn't stop smiling.

"It happened," Mattie said.

"It sure did. That was…. I have no words. You were crying. I could see how much he hated to see it, how your words were crushing him. I could see the pain, the feelings, and then bam! He caved. He's been feeling the same as you all along."

Had he?

That kiss told me he had, but I'd wait and see what happened tomorrow night.

On my date.

With Ryan Warden.

"I have a date tomorrow night."

"You do." Julian smiled.

Mattie rolled his eyes, but he was smiling when we both did a little jig and cried out in joy.

CHAPTER TWENTY-THREE

WARDEN

I'd never in my damn life been nervous about seeing a woman before. Until then. I even felt like I could puke as I walked up to Emmie's front door. That kiss the night before had me staying up most of the night replaying it in my head.

What I'd also been replaying, and I wished I hadn't, had been her words. How she thought she wasn't enough for me. Christ, it nearly broke me to hear the sorrow in her voice as she spoke to me, thinking I deserved better than her scarred self. She didn't understand, but she would. I didn't give two fucks about her scars; she was stunning inside and out. The thought of how she got them twisted my gut, but seeing them on her wouldn't stop me from feeling something for her.

Like I'd told her, what held me back the most was her age.

Not only the worry of what people would say to her about being with a man my age, but what would she do if something happened to me on the job? It could crush her in a way I would never want to. It was something I'd have to bring up one day with her if this was going to work out.

I knocked on her door and heard Julian say, "You're supposed to make him wait a little bit before answering."

The door swung open. Emmie stood in the doorway, smiling up at me. Fuck, she couldn't wait. She wasn't one to play games. She was excited to see me. I could also tell she was nervous by the way the hand that wasn't holding the door rested over her stomach and how she shifted from one foot to another.

"Baby doll," I said softly.

"Hi," she whispered.

Fuck it.

Reaching out, I slid an arm around her waist and tugged her towards me. As soon as her hands hit my chest, I leaned in and pressed my lips against hers.

It was quick. If I'd made it longer and got a real taste of her, I'd want more time just tasting and claiming her mouth.

"You ready?" I asked, grinning down at her.

"Yes," she said, her voice soft and light.

"Say bye to Julian."

She didn't look away from me when she called, "Bye, Julian."

"Take care of our dove," he said.

I lifted my gaze, caught his, and nodded.

"Always," I told him.

He smiled, giving two thumbs up. Shaking my head, I stepped out of the doorway, taking Emmie's hand in mine. Julian moved forward to the door. I knew he'd take care of the place.

"You got everything you need?" I asked down to Emmie.

Her eyes widened. She turned back, and Julian was already holding out her purse. Her face heated as she pulled it onto her shoulder and faced me again. "Now I do," she said, then reached out to take my hand. A thrill shot to my cock.

As I led her down the walkway, I took in her clothes. The night was warm. I wore jeans and a tee, but Emmie was covered. She had on a long skirt, a top that covered her up to her neck, and a cardigan.

When we stopped at my car, I turned her in to me. "You look gorgeous, always would to me, but you gotta be boilin', baby doll." I reached for her cardigan. She paled and stepped back.

My hands flew up flat in front of me. "All right. Not yet."

Red blazed her cheeks, and her eyes shot to the ground. "I'm sorry, I...." She shook her head.

I got close and cupped the side of her neck. "Hey."

She looked up at me. Christ, she was tiny. The top of her head reached my collarbone. She opened her mouth and I knew it was to apologise again, but I pressed a quick kiss to her lips.

"Don't say sorry, baby doll."

"But—"

"Nah, darlin'. Nothin' about it. Let's have a good night, yeah?"

"I'd like that."

Stepping back, I opened her door and waited until she sat in and put her seat belt on before I closed it. I walked around the front, keeping an eye on her, thinking she looked damn good sitting in my car.

Christ, how'd I get so goddamn lucky that she wanted me?

I couldn't understand it, but I was glad for it.

She smiled over at me as I got in. I returned it, which made her smile grow. Chuckling, I shook my head and started the car. As we drove, I asked, "How's work?"

She spoke proudly of it. I listened to each word out of her mouth. She'd come out of that basement not really talking or looking at people, but now she gabbed like she wanted to and kept her gaze on me the whole time.

It was damn good to see.

"I think you need to tell this client to fuck off," I told her as I pulled up out the front of the restaurant. She had a difficult customer who Talon had passed on to her. The dick kept changing his mind on things. I knew Talon wouldn't give a shit if she wiped him clean. I wouldn't either since the fucker was a guy.

She laughed. "I can't do that. I like to finish what I start, even when they're a pain. Plus, I told him I would be getting paid for all these changes. He didn't argue with me. It's bound to happen again and again in the business. Not everyone will be happy with what I produce first up."

"They should be. You've got talent."

She blushed. "Thank you."

One day she'd get used to compliments without reacting or feeling like she needed to say thanks. I winked before I climbed out of the car. I narrowed my eyes at her playfully when I saw she'd already gotten out before I could get her door.

Tapping the end of her nose, I told her, "Next time, and all times from here on out, I get your door for you, darlin'."

"Um, okay." She nodded.

Shifting her out of the way, I closed her door and locked the car. Taking her hand in mine, which dwarfed hers, which I fucking liked, we made our way into the restaurant.

The maître d' stood behind his little desk at the front. "Hi, how may I help you both?"

"Table under Warden."

"Right this way, sir." He led us to a table in the corner near the window. Before he could, I pulled out Emmie's chair. Once she was in and I was seated, the guy said, "Your waiter's name is Steven. He'll be along shortly to take your drink order."

"Thanks," I said and picked up a menu. This type of place wasn't my usual. I preferred a pub or bar meal, but I wanted to take Emmie somewhere special for our first date.

Hell. First date.

I presumed there'd be more. No, I wanted there to be more.

She glanced over the menu to me, smiling. "What do you think you'll have?"

"Steak," I answered automatically. "You?"

"Hmm, I'm not sure yet."

"Hello, my name's Steven. Can I get you and your father a drink?"

My fingers dug into the menu. Emmie's eyes flashed wide at me. She turned to the waiter. "It's funny you presume he's my father when we look nothing alike."

"I'm sorry, miss. Your uncle?"

I ground my teeth together and dropped the menu to fist my hands so I didn't reach out and grab the kid. He looked sixteen and was staring down at Emerson with doe eyes.

Just as I was about to fucking say something, Emmie did. "Wrong again. This is our first date, and I'd like many more with this man, so if you're going to continue to serve us, do it without speaking before Ryan shoves his fist down your throat." She'd said it so damn calmly, I snorted from shock. She faced me. "Unless you'd like to go elsewhere?"

I shook my head. The punk wasn't going to ruin this for us. "No, but if the dickhead doesn't stop staring at you like that, or if he does anything to our food, I'll be bashing his head into the table," I told her with a smile, making sure to use the same calm voice she had.

Emmie smiled over at me. I glanced up at the kid to see him gulp and nod. "Two Cokes and some water. We'll order when you come back." He nodded again and quickly disappeared. "Fuckin' arsehole."

Emmie's hand slid across the table. I caught a few people looking at us. Probably wondering who we were to each other. Still, I took her hand, and then she said, "I know you're uncomfortable about our age difference, but I need you to know I don't care what they see when they look at us. They can think what they like. I just want you to be comfortable to be seen with me at your side."

"Baby doll, I am comfortable. Like having you across from me already. They can think what they want and I'll damn try not to let it get to me, but it'll take time."

She nodded. "I can accept that."

I chuckled. "Good to hear."

She sat back, slid her hand from mine, and picked up the menu again. I watched her read it and wondered once again what she saw in me.

"Why me, Emmie?"

She pulled her eyes up to me slowly. A blush took over her cheeks. "Sorry?"

"I'm older, and I know it's got nothing to do with money. Just don't get why you've picked me."

The dickhead arrived before she could answer and silently placed the drinks on the table. He straightened and took out a pen and pad. Emmie made her order, and then I gave him mine. Then he left.

Emmie reached for her water and took a sip. Her hand shook a little and I wondered if it was because she was nervous about answering. She cleared her throat, a throat where the heat had spread to. "It was only you since the day you moved in."

I jerked my head back in shock. "What?"

"I saw so many that day, helping you move in. A lot of the men from the Hawks, but…." She took another sip. "Um, when

I saw you, all I could focus on was, well, you. No one else registered to me."

Say what the fuck now?

"Serious?"

"Yes. It sounds bad, but I don't think it was." She coughed. "I did stop watching you for a while because I was worried it was for the wrong reason."

I picked up my drink. "What do you mean, darlin'?"

She leaned forward. "I liked watching you a lot because I was very attracted to you." Fuck me, my chest puffed. To stop my cocky smirk, I took a gulp of Coke. But she went on, and I didn't expect what she'd say. "Then I got very turned on when I saw you have sex with that woman. I wished it had been me."

I sprayed my drink over the table and Emmie, then coughed up what felt like a lung. I pounded my fist against my chest. "What?"

She patted at her face with her napkin. "I'm so sorry. I shouldn't have said that. Oh God, why did I say that? And it's our first date. I've just ruined it. I should have left it alone. But you asked." She threw her hand my way and then dabbed at the table with her napkin. "Really, it's your fault. I'm nervous, flustered, can't believe I'm here with you, and I felt comfortable, which I also couldn't believe, so I just said it." She glared up at me. "Why do you make me nervous and comfortable all at the same time?"

"Because you like me."

She paused her dabbing. The blush reappeared. "I'm sorry for—"

"Baby doll, don't want to hear it. I like the thought of you watchin' me because you're attracted to this mug."

"But I invaded your privacy."

"*That* we'll talk on another time. Still, want you to know for now so you don't stress, I get why you watched. I'm turned on to know you got off on watching me and wishin' it was you. But we'll talk more about it another day."

"Why?" she whispered.

I shifted in my seat and adjusted my hardened dick. "It's my understanding you've never been touched."

She looked everywhere but at me. Still, she shook her head.

"Then I want you to understand I'm gonna take my time in this. Already see this'll go somewhere between us, so we need to take it slow, get used to it. Already my body reacts to your looks, to what you say. It ain't really the place for that to be going on. Usually I wouldn't give a shit, but when we're taking this slow because I want this to last, then we gotta talk about that sorta stuff another time."

She looked shocked with her wide eyes, but also pleased with her small smile.

I chuckled. "Let's enjoy our first dinner together, yeah?"

"Yes, Ryan."

I'd take care of Emmie because she deserved it. We wouldn't rush into this. We'd take our time, make sure it'd last like I already felt I wanted it to deep down in my core. And she didn't seem fazed that I'd told her that either.

Goddamn, I was a lucky motherfucker.

*M*y feelings for Ryan were cemented inside of me. It had only been a couple of months, but I knew I was completely in love with him. If it was crazy, then so be it, but every time I called him, saw him, my heartbeat shot straight to erratic. Even if I got a text from him, I would smile, my body would warm, and happiness consumed me.

We'd shouted at each other a few times over stupid things, but I always felt safe, felt like I could be myself. I wanted to share my opinion, even if he didn't agree with it.

He could annoy me, make me angry, but I still loved him.

I hadn't told him, and I wasn't sure he was ready to hear it. I wasn't even sure I was ready to share it.

No matter, I knew how I felt and was happy.

I glanced at myself in the mirror. I was back to the weight I had been and more. Since Ryan was showing any moment to pick me up for a lunch date and the weather was still warm, I dressed in a light sleeveless summer dress.

Ryan had taught me to love myself. He gave me the strength

to do so and not care about what other people thought. Of course, it took time to come to that conclusion, and I struggled along the way, but I got there. It was also so Ryan would promise to try and stop worrying about the age difference. He'd brought up how concerned he was about it, and his worry about if something happened to him, and he left me alone. He didn't want to tell me at first, but he confessed it late one night when we'd been lying in bed together. I'd rolled into him and told him how I couldn't waste my time worrying about something that *could* happen. I wanted to enjoy the time we had together, no matter how long it was. No one could predict the future, so it was best to make the most of it.

He'd tucked my hair behind my ear and said, "Okay, baby doll." He'd rolled me more on top of him, where I *felt* how he liked me on there, and had distracted me with a kiss soon after.

I loved our nights together, no matter if it was at my place or his. Going to sleep at his side, tucked close, had me gushing just thinking of it... but I wanted more.

I wanted him.

I'd tried a couple of times earlier on to get us to move forward, but in that area, he kept me at arm's length. He never shied away from affection. He enjoyed as much as I did showing how we cared by touching, hugging, and kissing. Even if people were around.

It was time to kick this relationship up a notch.

We stood on his back deck talking before bed. A deck I'd been apprehensive to go onto because it was in view of the basement window. A room I never wanted to remember. However, as Ryan eased me out the first time, I realised, even when my stomach rolled and body tensed, Ryan was there. He was this me and that nightmare would be just that from then on. A nightmare I would eventually get over.

Ryan stepped up and slid his arms around my waist, bringing my thoughts back into the present. My hands wrapped over his arms and I rested my head back.

"We're dating, right?"

I tilted my head to the side to see his lips twitching. "Yeah, baby doll, we're datin'."

A gasp burst from my chest when he swept me up into his arms and carried me up to his room. Finally.

Once on the bed, he locked my travelling hands between just one of his large ones above my head.

"You gonna stop?" he asked.

"Sure," I said, then bit my bottom lip to stop from smiling.

He didn't believe me. He chuckled, kissed me deeply, and rolled into me more. His free hand glided over my breast, causing me to suck in a breath. He pulled his lips from mine and his dark eyes locked onto my gaze. "You hurtin', darlin'?"

I tilted my head in confusion. "Hurtin'?"

He smirked. "Aching, baby doll. You wantin' to come?"

Understanding dawned on me. "Um, yes." My body shivered from the thought of it.

"Then let me help you." He kissed me again, only to stop. "Tell me if you don't like anythin' I do."

A snort slipped out. I said, "I doubt that will happen."

"Promise me, Emmie."

As soon as his hand loosened from my wrists, I wrapped my arms around his neck. "Okay, Ryan."

"Good. Now put your hands back. No touchin'. Gonna make you feel good, baby doll." When I didn't move right away, because my clit was crying in joy, he ordered again, "Hands up, darlin'."

I did, as I doubted my body would forgive me for missing out on what was to come.

His lips touched down on my neck. Immediately, I arched it, only to freeze when they glided over my scars on my chest. "Baby, you're beautiful," he murmured.

I relaxed, only a little, until his mouth reached my nipple. He bit down on it over my clothes. With a gasp, I latched onto his head, wanting to keep him there.

"Hands," he growled.

I forced them back up and gripped the metal poles on the headboard.

He moved, hiked up enough to grab my tee at each side of my waist and pulled it up. I shifted so he could drag it all the way off.

His heated gaze zeroed in on my breasts covered by my bra. He didn't bother undoing it. Instead, he gripped the top of one cup and pulled it down, exposing my breast to him. His eyes lifted to mine. They held questions. He was worried he'd scared me or that he'd moved too fast.

He was wrong.

Smiling, I nodded. A puff of breath escaped his mouth before he slid down to his elbow on the bed and hovered half over me. First, he kissed just above my nipple. His tongue came out to play and he licked all the way around the areola before he sucked my nipple into his mouth. I gasped, my hips jutting up and rubbing against him. He groaned as he swirled his tongue around my hardened nipple. He covered that one up and then pulled the other side of my bra down to pay it just as much slow attention as he had to the first.

By the time he lifted his head, grinning, I panted, "More?"

"Christ, yes," he said, covering my breast with my bra. "Gotta make my woman cry my name." He kissed my stomach and it quivered under his lips. I felt him smile against my skin. Lower again he went and kissed just the top of my jeans. His fingers grazed my exposed skin as he undid the button. A needy shiver ripped through my body and he glanced up, but I was already nodding. He chuckled and slowly unzipped my jeans.

Unfortunately, he climbed off the bed next.

"Ryan?"

"Relax, baby doll. I'm comin' back." He removed his tee and then his jeans, and my breath caught. I'd always admired his bulky form, but to have it and see it up close was even better. I made to climb out of bed, wanting to touch him, but he shook his head. "Don't move, darlin'. Lift up for a sec." I curled up as he pulled the sheet down, then lay back and lifted my bottom so he could move the sheet all the way. He climbed back into bed and tugged the sheet over us. When his hands went to my jeans and he pulled them free, along with my panties, I was glad he'd covered us.

"Wasn't sure how you felt about bein' fully naked in front of me yet, baby." That was sweet. I'd never been naked around a man before, and I wasn't sure I was ready for it just yet. I was even glad I still had my bra on. His concern warmed me.

Reaching over, I ran a hand through his hair. His eyes lifted to mine. "You're very thoughtful."

He winked. "Don't tell anyone."

I smiled. "I won't."

Next, his hand circled my stomach. My pulse spiked, knowing he had easy access to my parts below. "You still want this? We can stop anytime you want."

"I want it, please. But…."

"What, baby doll?"

"Can, ah, I touch you?"

"Yeah, darlin'."

Since he was on his side and I was on my back right next to

him, though we weren't touching except for his hand on my stomach, I slid my hand out and cupped his cock behind his boxers.

"Whoa," he growled out. "I... fuck, you wanna touch my cock?"

I dipped my brows. "Well, yes."

"Shit, sorry, didn't expect it. Thought you meant my body, minus my dick, while I pleasure you."

I'd shocked him. I liked that I had. A laugh escaped me before I sobered and made sure. "So you don't mind?"

He gulped. I watched his Adam's apple bounce up and down. "No. You can do whatever you want to me."

I licked my suddenly dry lips. "You'll tell me if I do anything wrong?"

His forehead hit mine. "Yeah, baby doll." He kissed me. I opened my lips under his and touched my tongue to his. Slowly, I placed my hand against his hard, so very hard cock and stroked up and down on it. His hips shifted forward, so he must have liked that.

I couldn't believe how firm he was. I'd heard stories, seen things from health class at school back in the day, but I'd never experienced anything. The only orgasm I'd had was by my own hand.

Spreading my legs felt natural when Ryan's hand slid lower. His fingers glided through my pubic hair, and on the first touch of his finger against my clit, I gasped. My head dug back into the pillow, my hips jutting forward, wanting more of his touch.

"Baby doll, you're so wet for me," he whispered into my ear as he slid two fingers down to circle my opening. I nodded against his shoulder, shielding my burning face. "Look at me, darlin'," he ordered, his voice deeper and rougher than normal.

With a gulp of strength, I pulled my head back and met his hot gaze. "You feel so damn good, baby."

I gripped my hand tighter around him, and he grunted. Even though I was embarrassed for being so turned on, having Ryan talk eased some of it. I told him, "So do you."

"You mind if I lick you here, darlin'?" He glided his finger up and down my slit.

My body quivered. "R-really?"

"Yeah, baby doll. I'd love to taste you."

Too nervous to say what I wanted, I nodded. He kissed me and nipped my bottom lip, slowly dragging it from between his teeth while holding my eyes. With another peck of my lips, he trailed kisses to my chest, my shoulders, my arms. Tears sprang to my eyes. He was showing me my scars didn't bother him.

He kissed down my stomach, then pulled the sheet up over his head. The grip on my thighs as he spread me open made me groan. My heart couldn't slow. I tried to calm it by taking bigger breaths, but it wasn't working. Instead, I gave up and let myself get lost in Ryan and his fingers and mouth. Especially when his large frame slid between my open legs. I covered my face and bit my bottom lip. While I knew I shouldn't have been embarrassed by him seeing me like that, I was.

Only when he kissed my thighs over and over, and tears welled and fell, did I pull my hands away from my face. He ran his large hands up, over, and around my legs, caressing me.

I was dumbfounded by how the scars truly didn't bother him. He touched them like he didn't care they were there. He made me like them.

But then all thought dropped from my mind when his warm breath brushed against me. Between my legs. His lips pressed against my clit. A noise dropped from my mouth. Holy moly, I liked how that felt. Even better was when he licked from my clit down and then back up. He groaned. I didn't know why, but it vibrated against me and had me gripping the sheet. I wanted to lock his head between my legs. I wanted to grab his hair and drive myself up onto his face, but I didn't. Instead, Ryan hooked his hands under my bottom and lifted me onto his face more. His mouth, tongue, teeth, and lips went crazy up and down, all over me.

"Ryan," I cried. Already my orgasm built. That sweet, wonderful feeling spread through my lower belly. "Ryan," I begged, wanting and needing more. I just didn't know what.

His lips pressed against my clit again, but then he knifed himself up, hovered over me. "Trust me?" he asked.

"Of course," I replied, my throat dry from panting.

His hand between us moved around. I didn't know what he was doing until I felt something pressed against my clit. My eyes widened. "Is that...? Are we going to...?"

"Not yet, baby doll, but one day soon. Tonight, we're both gonna come though."

"O-okay." I nodded. When he gently slid his dick over my clit, I gasped. It felt like his finger, but better because I knew, from the heated look in his eyes, he liked the feeling too.

Reaching up, I used my hand behind his neck to tug him down. He landed over me, and he kept rubbing against me over and over, my thighs secured around his waist, gliding with him up and down. I chased his lips, but he didn't give them to me right away. "Baby, I taste you on my tongue still."

"I don't care," I told him, and I didn't. Once again my insides were firing up, ready to explode. He groaned and planted his mouth on mine. I held him tightly. "Ryan," I mumbled against his lips.

"Right here. Right with you," he said, his forehead pressing down into my shoulder. His hand slid under my arse and he pulled me up against him more. "Christ," he clipped.

I slammed my eyes shut when my clit pulsed and I came, screaming, "Ryan."

"Yes. Fuck yes, darlin'." Warmth spread between us, over my mound and stomach as Ryan groaned low in his throat.

CHAPTER TWENTY-FIVE

EMERSON

A knock on my front door brought me out of my thoughts of the night I spent with Ryan. I knew I was probably flushed from them, but I still raced into the living room and to the door. Without checking who it was, as I was expecting Ryan, I opened it.

My smile faded. "Harriet," I whispered.

Tears welled in her eyes as they moved over my scars. "I'm sorry," she blurted before burying her head into her hands.

I moved without thinking about it. I wrapped my arms around her and hugged her close as she cried.

"I'm sorry," Harriet mumbled again.

"You have nothing to be sorry for. I'm the one who's sorry. I should have contacted you sooner."

She sniffed and wiped at her face. "No, I understand why you didn't."

Smiling gently, I asked, "Why don't you come in?"

Her smile was wonky, but she nodded. "I'd like that."

With an arm around her waist, I led her into the living room. We sat together on the couch. Surprise flittered through me that I wasn't nervous to be around her. Maybe it was because I already knew her and liked her from years ago.

"I shouldn't have believed the lies," she said softly.

She didn't know better; they'd been good lies. It had all come out in court. How my aunt had told Harriet I moved to the new school to get away. She'd made the impression that Donny had tried to rape me, so I wanted to get away from him and from the friend who'd set us up in the first place. The police had visited looking for Donny after he disappeared. Only they didn't look too far into it after his mum had found a suicide note stating how he regretted so much in life. Gloria and her people made out that he'd raped and killed a girl. The letter told the police where to find the body. Of course, the police believed the note when it did lead to a body. Apparently the girl who looked very similar to me had been questioned by the police about Donny. She cried and told them of the horrid night he took her out on a date. She confessed it was all a lie in the end. What hurt the most was that Donny's mum never knew the truth. She died from cancer not long after her son's death.

"I'd been hurt thinking Donny would do that and how you could blame me for it. W-when they found his note, I... I lost it. I didn't know what was real and what wasn't. I eventually climbed out of that pit. But then all this came to light and...."

"You didn't know what to do or say?" She nodded. "I didn't either, and I don't still. I wanted to reach out to you so many times."

"You saved me and my family from *her* and those others."

"You would have done the same."

"I don't know if I could have."

"I do."

She shook her head. "I'm sorry for not coming sooner. I mean, I've been trying for the last month, but that lady at the private investigation firm, Violet, kept putting me off. She said you were getting your life together."

I honestly didn't expect that. I wasn't sure why Violet held Harriet back, but I did appreciate the thought.

"I am. I have." I smiled, thinking of Ryan and my business, my house and my friends.

"So…" She licked her lips. "Do you think you would do an interview with me for channel ten?"

I stiffened, my throat thickening. "Sorry?" I asked, just as the front door opened. Ryan stepped in and closed the door behind him. His eyes narrowed on Harriet. I should have known it hadn't been Ryan at the door earlier; he wouldn't have knocked since he had a key, and if it was open, he would just walk in. Still, if I'd have looked first, I had a feeling I would have opened the door to Harriet anyway.

But regret tightened my stomach.

She wasn't really at my house just for an interview… right?

"Get the fuck out," Ryan snarled.

"Ryan?" I said, standing from the couch.

He crossed his arms over his chest and lifted his chin Harriet's way. "This bitch is only after one thing, a payday. She's been hounding all of us at the firm for your address and number, sayin' shit about missin' you and wantin' your friendship back. But we weren't born fuckin' yesterday. We never gave it because we'd heard all the damn TV stations have promised her big money if she got you in for an interview."

"That's not true," Harriet cried, standing next to me. She took my hand, but I quickly pulled it free.

"Bullshit," Ryan clipped. "Violet just rang, said she'd been in there this mornin' and when a client came in bein' a dick, Harriet disappeared, but the file drawer had been opened." His eyes caught mine. "Usually it's locked tight, but Violet had just been in it when this bitch made an appearance. Know it's no excuse, but it won't happen again. Violet's fuckin' fumin'. She's in the process of takin' all the case files into the lockdown room where no one can get to them without a goddamn security card and access number."

Why Violet had stopped Harriet's visit made sense now.

Anger had me facing Harriet and demanding, "Get out."

"What? No! You have to do this," she snapped. "You owe me this. My world wouldn't have been messed up if it wasn't for you."

"I'm sorry?" I asked, appalled. "Are you telling me you were beaten, threatened, had people murdered in front of you just because you wanted to go home? Did you witness a girl younger than we had been back then being raped, drugged?" I yelled, my breath heavy. "Did your aunt slice at your skin over and over?" I waved my arm in her face. I took a deep breath to calm my erratic heart. "She did it all because her boyfriend stared at you like he was going to fuck you. Did that happen to you? Do I owe you for any of that? For being locked away for over two years of your life in a basement?" In the earlier days, I would have caved. I would have seen her misfortune, whatever it had been, as my fault. I would have done things I didn't want to do to please her. But I wasn't the same person any longer.

I had love in my life. People who cared.

I was strong.

No one would bully me into something I didn't want to do. No one could control me any longer.

I had the strength to stand up for myself.

Stepping into her, so her face was close to mine, I told her, "Get the fuck out before I sic Ryan on you."

Her eyes widened. She glanced over at Ryan, who I heard open the door. Harriet nodded, stepped back, and then walked around the coffee table. I watched her go and waited until she was out the door with Ryan closing it before I relaxed.

Only the tension rolled back in and I started to pace while I ranted, "Can you believe her? I mean, really, the nerve. She hasn't been through anything. She got to stay in her cosy little house with her parents. I owe her nothing. The greedy... greedy—"

"Whore," Ryan offered.

I waved my hand at him. "Yes, that." I stopped and faced him. Dread surfaced. "I don't owe her, right? I mean, she could be upset about everything that went down. Especially with how Donny died. They were friends. She could blame me. And it is my fault."

Ryan stalked towards me. His hands cupped my face and drew my gaze to his. "It's not your fuckin' fault. What happened to the guy, to that neighbour, wasn't your fault. It was on that cunt and motherfucker you lived with. It's their fault. Their sick and twisted minds. You owe that bitch nothing. She's a money-hungry slut who saw a quick way to earn some cash through you. Don't let her get to you."

"Okay," I whispered. His words were fierce, hard, and if it was anyone else, the tone would have me cringing in fear. Instead, I was trembling in need.

His eyes widened from whatever he saw, his jaw clenched, and he told me, "We're goin' to my house for lunch. Pack a bag. You're stayin' the night."

It was lucky for him that his ordering me didn't bother me. I stood up for myself when I needed to and didn't like his tone. But right then, *I* wanted to go to Ryan's house. *I* wanted to have lunch with him before he went back to work, and then that night, after he'd come home, I would also get what *I* wanted.

Him. Naked. In bed with me.

I could read he wanted me as much as I did. He held back for a reason that was no longer an issue—to give us time, to get used to us dating. He didn't want to rush because what we had was something important to him. Tonight though, he'd have to understand I was over waiting.

He was important to me, and I wanted to show him in every way I could.

"Jesus, woman. Whatever you're thinkin', stop before I strip you bare and take you on the damn floor."

Bug-eyed, I asked, "How was I looking?" because I wanted to do it again.

His arms slid around my waist and I wrapped mine around his shoulders. Ryan leaned down and nipped at my ear before saying, "Like you want to eat me for lunch."

"Is that an option?" I breathed.

He stilled and then stepped away from me. "Bag. Now."

I couldn't help but pout.

He cursed. "Baby doll, we'll talk about that over lunch."

"Sex," I wanted to clarify.

He groaned. "Yes," he hissed.

"As in when we'll be having sex with each other," I pushed.

"Emerson," he clipped.

I bit my bottom lip to keep from smiling and walked past him with a new sway to my hips. It seemed Ryan's resistance was crashing like mine had been for a while.

I had a feeling I would definitely be getting some Ryan Warden tonight.

All I had to do was get through lunch, watch him go back to work, and try and concentrate on my own jobs while I waited for him to get back from work.

Maybe I could cook something special for the occasion. But what did one cook when they were going to lose their virginity?

CHAPTER TWENTY-SIX

EMERSON

*O*nce at Ryan's house, he dropped my bag just inside the door before shutting it. I stood there for a moment, and like usual, my eyes drifted to the bottom of the stairs. I took a moment to feel the loss of Mrs Minna. Ryan gave it to me, like always. When I'd first started coming to his house, I wasn't sure how I felt about knowing her body had laid on the floor, but time, reassurance, and kind words from Ryan helped.

He stepped up behind me, his hands on my shoulders. He rubbed them down my arms. His lips met my neck before he moved off through the living room and then into the kitchen. He was giving me time. Only I didn't need as much as I used to. Life had to go on. I couldn't change the past. Instead, I had to live in the present.

Turning, I kicked off my shoes beside Ryan's and went into the kitchen. I gasped when I saw he had the table laid with a lunch made for two. There were candles, a tablecloth, two plates, containers full of different types of food and a bottle of wine. Though, I also caught the beer bottle for Ryan.

Moving to him, I wound my arms around his waist. "This is beautiful."

He ran his hands up and down my back. "Glad you like it, baby doll."

I pulled my head back. Responding to the invite, Ryan leaned down and pressed his lips against mine quickly. "Let's eat."

"Sounds good and smells good. Did you make it all?"

With his hand to my lower back, he led me to the table and pulled out my chair. "It's just cold chicken, darlin'. Some salads, bread, and cakes. Nothin' hard."

I smiled, sitting and waited for him to sit across from me. "That didn't answer my question."

Did my eyes deceive me? I was sure Ryan's cheeks reddened a little. He grabbed his beer, twisted the cap off and before he took a gulp, he said, "Yeah, I made it."

He'd taken his time to prepare the meal for me. There were at least three different slices, and a cake. Happiness filled me; I felt giddy by it.

If my dad had met Ryan, he would have loved him for me.

"Thank you," I whispered, my voice thick with emotions.

His eyes softened. "You're welcome, baby doll."

As we ate, we spoke of Harriet, but I quickly steered it away. I didn't want either of us to get back to work feeling furious. Yes, I hadn't known her long at school, but I would never have picked her to be a user, a fake. I'd thought she honestly was happy and concerned for me, but it was an act to get something from me.

"Emmie, you said not to think of it." Ryan grinned.

I rolled my eyes. "I can't help it."

"I know… how about I take your mind off it?"

My head tilted to the side in confusion. "I thought you had to go back to work?"

"Got the afternoon off."

"Really?"

"Yeah. You busy or can you take some time off as well?"

I did have to finish a design… but alone time with Ryan was what I wanted. Alone time in bed with Ryan would be better. I couldn't get the other night from my mind, the feel of him between my legs, how he made my body tremble in pleasure.

"Emmie," he called. His mouth twitched in humour. Could he read my mind?

My face heated. "Yes, um, I can free up the afternoon. What did you have in mind?"

He played with the beer bottle on the table while watching me. "Can't stop thinkin' about the other night."

Yes! I wasn't the only one.

"And?"

His lips twitched again. "Come here, Emmie," he ordered, his voice deeper than usual. I stood and walked around the table. Ryan scooted his chair back. Once I stood before him, he took my hands in his and gently tugged me forward. My legs opened, going on each side of his thighs as I straddled his lap. My dress tugged up, just covering my panties.

Ryan placed his hands on my thighs and ran them up and down, ignoring my scars. I put my hands on his shoulders.

"You enjoyed the other night, right?" he asked. I nodded. "You been wantin' more though, haven't you?"

"Yes," I whispered. My clit throbbed while my pulse ticked heavily at the side of my neck.

"I wanna give my woman more, baby doll, but we know it's your first time. You know it's gonna hurt, right?"

I nodded again. "But if it's with you, my first time will still be something special."

"Fuck," he clipped. He cupped the back of my neck and pulled me down. His lips hit mine. It wasn't a soft, sweet kiss.

It was demanding and hard. With a firm grip on my arse cheeks, he dragged me closer, making my pussy rub against his hardness. The contact sent a shiver throughout me, so I did it again and again.

His lips travelled down my neck, and I arched back for him. He kissed and bit at my shoulder. There, he rumbled out, "Undo my jeans, baby doll."

My stomach swirled, and even though my hands trembled from nerves and excitement, I moved back a little and slid them between us. Ryan kept kissing and nipping at my skin as he ran the strap of my dress down from my shoulder.

I undid his button and then slid his zipper down.

"Take my cock out, darlin'."

Panting, I reached under his jeans and boxers and gripped his cock. I gently pulled him free and stared down at his dick. He was thick and long. Mesmerised, I ran my hand up and down his length.

"Christ, baby doll. Love you touchin' me."

"I love touching you."

His hips jutted up, revealing the tip of his cock, which leaked. "You want this inside you?"

I nodded.

"Words, Emmie."

Lifting my head, I met his dark gaze. "Yes. I want you inside of me. Be my first, Ryan."

He pulled my hand away from his dick and his eyes hardened. He cupped my jaw tightly. Leaning in to me, he stated, "First, last, and *only*, baby doll."

"Yes, Ryan."

"Good," he grunted. A moment later, he stood with me in his arms. I let out a squeal from the sudden movement, but I wrapped around him close and held on as he took us through the living room, up the stairs, and into his bedroom. There he let my legs fall and my feet hit the floor. He tangled his fingers through my hair and bent, kissing me with so much passion and need it left me breathless.

His fingers slid the other side of my sundress off my shoulder so he could kiss me there. The whole time I gripped his tee at his waist. Nerves had my heart galloping when I felt his finger at the zipper on the back of my dress. Air whooshed out of me as he eased it down.

He stepped back and the dress fell to the floor, leaving me in panties since I hadn't worn a bra with the dress.

"Fuck," he bit out. His dick jerked as his eyes ate me up. "Goddamn beautiful, baby doll."

Before his words, I wanted to cover myself, feeling self-conscious. After them, I placed my thumbs into each side of my panties and dragged them down my legs. Ryan sucked in a sharp breath when I straightened before him. The next moment, he lifted his tee from his body and threw it to the floor. He pulled off his socks hurriedly and went for his jeans, but I said, "C-can I take them off you?"

His hands dropped to his sides. "You can do anythin', darlin'."

With a soft smile, I stepped up to him, met his eyes, and kissed his chest before I took hold of his jeans and boxers and pulled them down slowly. His dick jerked again when I bent down to help him step out of them. I stood and took all of him in.

Amazing.

"You're so handsome," I told him.

"Glad you think so, baby doll." He curled an arm around my waist and drew me into his space. My chest hit his. We both made a noise in the backs of our throats. "Gotta get you ready for me, darlin'."

"Okay," I whispered. His hand travelled to cup my mound. Instinctively, my hips jerked forward, liking his touch.

His finger glided up and down my slit. "Christ, you're already wet."

"For you."

"Fuckin' love it." He kissed me again. I wrapped my arms around his neck and held on. "Spread a little," he said against my lips before claiming my mouth once again. I stepped out, opening up for him as he eased a finger inside of me. I whimpered into his mouth; he growled back in response. Another finger joined the first and my knees shook. I tightened my hold on him and he held me securely to his side with his other arm around my waist.

A third finger dipped in. "So fuckin' tight. So good." The heel of his hand brushed against my clit, and a moan escaped from my lips onto his.

But then his fingers disappeared. He picked me up and took the few steps to the bed to lay me on it with him hovering over me. My poor heart was in a tizzy while my body ached with need. I wanted him in me.

Ryan leaned away and got to his knees. He grabbed each of my legs and ran his hands up and down them. I shivered. He lifted one leg higher and kissed my calf before he did the same to the other. Next, he spread my thighs wide to fit his form between them.

"Glistenin'," he said roughly, staring down at my pussy. "Should've mentioned earlier, but I'm clean, baby doll. Need to know, are you on the pill? Wanna go bareback with my woman, but if you're not protected against gettin' pregnant, I'll cover it."

My cheeks were on fire, but I managed to answer, "I'm good. On the pill."

Satisfaction made his smile a big one. "Perfect," he growled.

He leaned forward. One hand went to the bed by my waist, the other he used to spread my labia apart. He pressed a finger against my clit and my hips jerked up. I bit my bottom lip and breathed heavily through my nose.

He glided his finger lower and circled my entrance. "You wanna take me in here?"

I nodded. His hand fell away and he climbed up my body. A hand landed beside my head. His other I felt between us. I lifted my head to see him stroking himself. His tip kept hitting my clit and a needy little growl fell from my lips.

"All right, baby girl. You'll get me." The tip of his cock slipped down easily through my excitement and stopped just outside of me. "Hold on to me, darlin'."

Nerves fluttered through my belly, but I eagerly wrapped my hands around his upper arms, as much as I could anyway. Ryan pushed in a little and I gasped. The sense of being filled hit me, and when he pushed in a little more, my breath was taken again.

He stopped, and I glanced up at him. His jaw clenched and sweat formed on his forehead. I lifted my hips a little in invitation, which was all he needed. With a swift thrust forward, he embedded inside of me. I cried out, tears forming in my eyes, my pussy throbbing from the harsh sting.

Ryan didn't move. He breathed deeply but didn't move. "You okay, baby?"

"Just, um, give me a second."

He leaned down and I winced a little. But when he started kissing me, I forgot about the pain. I lifted my legs, planted my feet to the bed and hugged his waist with my thighs. Ryan groaned, and a pleased smile appeared on my lips as he trailed kisses along my jaw, to my neck and shoulder. I wanted to hear his groan again, but when his hand rounded my breast and gently caressed it, I got lost in the moment and rocked my hips up. It was then he sucked in a sharp breath. It told me he liked my action. So I did it again. I was rewarded with a grunted curse before he slammed his lips back to mine.

"Ryan," I said against them. I felt I needed more.

He read it and said, "Gonna move inside you, baby doll."

"Please," I whispered.

Slowly, he pulled back, rolling his hips around gently. It stung a little, but when he pressed down on my clit, rubbing up and down, while pushing back in, the sensation changed.

"Ryan," I cried. My thighs squeezed him tighter as he ground down into me, moving his finger and using his body to press in the right place. Wide-eyed, I gasped when my lower stomach tingled. "Ryan," I breathed.

"Yeah, baby doll." His thrusts picked up, in and out of me, then grinding down on me faster and harder. His hand around my breast, his grip harder than usual, he dipped his head and sucked a nipple into his mouth.

"Yes," I cried. My walls clenched around his cock as it pushed in and out of me. "Ryan. God, Ryan."

"That's it, darlin'. Fuck yes, keep comin' on my cock." His mouth hit mine. My hands glided down his back to his butt cheeks, where I squeezed. Ryan groaned low into my mouth. He pulled back enough to clip, "Christ, fuck, gonna come. Now." His harsh grunts hit the room. He slowed his thrusts to a leisurely drift in and out.

Nothing could have made this moment between us more perfect than it was.

Ryan brushed my hair from my face and lightly pinched my chin. "You feel so fuckin' perfect."

So did he.

Leaning up, I kissed him.

My world wouldn't have been the same if he hadn't moved

into this house. I'd been out to find freedom, and I had. But how lucky was I that I'd found it with a man I loved.

"This is amazing," I told him with a lazy smile.

"Yeah?"

"Definitely."

"Good, baby doll." Gently, he pulled out of me and shifted off the bed. I caught sight of some blood and cringed. "Nah-uh, darlin'. Don't you worry about anythin'." He opened his en-suite door, came back to the bed, and picked me up, bridal style, in his arms. Laughing, I rested my head against his chest. When we entered the bathroom, I saw the bath full of water already.

I lifted my gaze to his. "Made it extra hot before I came to get you. Should be good now."

"So your plan was to have me all along?"

"Fuck yes."

Laughing again, I slapped his chest. "I'm glad."

"Nah, baby doll. I'm glad you wanted me."

EPILOGUE

EMERSON

*R*yan walked with me tucked under his arm into the compound common room. They'd decided to throw a party just because they wanted to. Still, I thought it had something to do with a going-away party for Blue and Clary, who'd I'd met recently at their wedding.

However, I realized I was mistaken when I didn't even see Blue or Clary. Instead, it was a small crowd of Talon, Zara, Ivy, Killer, Julian, and Mattie, plus a couple of prospects to serve us dinner and drinks. When Julian had told me about the party, I honestly didn't expect this, but I enjoyed it. Sitting beside Ryan all night while talking with Zara, Julian, and Ivy was something I hoped we would do all the time.

I would even like to try my hand at a dinner party at Ryan's place, since his was bigger than mine and I loved cooking in his open plan kitchen.

This was comfortable. Almost like we were all part of the same family. It felt like home, especially because of the man at my side.

Ryan caught me looking at him. He smiled, leaned in to

take my lips in a quick but fierce kiss, and said, "Be back in a sec."

"All right." I nodded and watched him walk away towards the bar.

"Hey, dovey dove. Have you seen the sign Talon put up with your logo on it?"

I sucked in a breath. "It's up?" I asked, looking from Julian to Talon.

Talon chuckled. "Yeah, darlin'. Fuckin' finally got around to it. Go see your awesome design. The guys sure do love it."

"I'm so glad." I stood and met Julian at the end of the table they'd set up. I glanced back. "Does anyone else want to come?"

Ivy waved her hand. "You two go. Zara and I'll get dessert ready."

Smiling, I nodded. Ivy had talked about her chocolate and banana cheesecake all night and I couldn't wait to try it.

Julian led me through the compound. He turned on lights as we walked so it was easier to see. In through the workshop and then out the front door of it. With his arm around my shoulders, we walked a few paces away from the front and turned back. I looked up and my breath caught. The sign looked amazing. I'd incorporated a tire, wings to represent the Hawks, and the business name all together. It looked amazing above the roller doors, lit up so all could see.

"Do you like it?"

"I do. It looks so much better with how big they made the sign."

"It does." We stood there and talked about some other clients I had. How business had picked up even more and how Julian found it cute that I had a desk set up at both my place and Ryan's. Ryan and I spent so much time together that when I had to get work done at his place, I was sick of sitting in the kitchen when he would be in the living room.

Eventually, we walked back inside. I asked how things were going for Mattie and Zara's sister—well, foster sister—living in Melbourne. I hadn't met her or their parents, but I knew of them. I still found comfort in smaller crowds which contained women I already knew. Slowly I'd built myself up to meet new people.

"We're not too sure. When we call, she doesn't say much. Actually we're starting to worry about her. I think Nancy will end up doing something soon."

"It's a big change, moving to a place where she doesn't know anyone. It might take a while for her to get used to it."

"Yeah, maybe." He opened the door back into the common room. I walked by him and froze.

Julian stepped up behind me and led me closer to where Ryan sat with a guitar on his knee and a microphone in front of him.

"You know I don't do this shit in front of anyone. But this was a special occasion, so people are gonna have to listen to me whether they like it or not."

I couldn't speak. I managed a nod, but all I could do was watch as Ryan strummed his first chord.

Right away the music hit me. It was the first song he'd played me. "Beautiful Crazy." His voice hit the room through the microphone, and I couldn't understand why, but him singing this time was better than the first.

His voice, a low rumble that caused my body to melt, had tears welling. I clasped my hands on the front of my chin, a couple of fingers pressing down on my trembling lips.

He was amazing.

An arm slid around my waist. I glanced at Ivy quickly but then straight back at Ryan.

"He's wonderful," Ivy said.

I nodded. Gently we swayed to his words, about being beautiful crazy, taking chances, and wearing hearts on sleeves.

His eyes never left me. Every word sang to me.

They hit me soul deep, and I had no doubt he meant those words for me.

How my crazy was beautiful to him.

How I amazed him.

When the song came to an end, he put his guitar on the floor, stood, and came for me. Julian and Ivy moved away. Ryan stopped right in front of me.

"Did you like it, baby doll?"

It wasn't pretty, but I sniffed and wiped at my eyes, probably spreading mascara everywhere. "More than words can say."

He chuckled and gently ran a finger under my eyes. His gaze met mine. "Want you livin' with me, Emmie."

Awestruck, I blinked slowly. "A-are you asking me to move in with you?"

His smile was sweet. "Yeah, baby doll."

I gulped and nodded.

"Words, darlin'."

"Yes. Yes, Ryan, I would love to move in with you."

"Fuck yes," he clipped, and then kissed me.

We weren't the perfect couple. We argued, got mad, but we were us. And moving forward in life together was what mattered most to me. I couldn't wait for our future because there was no way Ryan Warden was getting rid of me now.

"I love you, Ryan Warden," I said against his lips.

His arms curled around me tightly. "Love you, Emmie. Always."

ACKNOWLEDGMENTS

Never would I have thought my characters to be accepted so well where readers want to hear about *all* of them. Warden had always been a side character. I've always loved him and enjoyed writing his small scenes in the other books, but I didn't think I'd have it in me to write a full-length…. I'm so grateful to my readers wanting his story, because I'm in love with Warden even more than I had been. Emmie has also stolen a piece of my heart!

Becky and her kickass team at Hot Tree Editing. Becky, I love working with you each and every time. I wouldn't give you up for anything, and I hope you know you're never getting rid of me.

Craig, Shayla, and Jake, thank you for getting out of my hair when I needed to write since my office is in the living room… for now.

Leah, thank you for your friendship. If you didn't get me out of the house, I wouldn't go anywhere. Thank you for listening, always being there, and yes, for even being a pain in the butt.

Lindsey and Amanda, I adore you both for being my beta readers, but not only that, for your honesty as well.

Wander and Andrey, thank you both for listening to me about a character and finding me the perfect cover photo every time.

ALSO BY LILA ROSE

Hawks MC: Ballarat Charter
Holding Out (FREE) Zara and Talon
Climbing Out: Griz and Deanna
Finding Out (novella) Killer and Ivy
Black Out: Blue and Clarinda
No Way Out: Stoke and Malinda
Coming Out (novella) Mattie and Julia

Hawks MC: Caroline Springs Charter
The Secret's Out: Pick, Billy and Josie
Hiding Out: Dodge and Willow
Down and Out: Dive and Mena
Living Without: Vicious and Nary
Walkout (novella) Dallas and Melissa
Hear Me Out: Beast and Knife
Breakout (novella) Handle and Della
Fallout: Fang and Poppy

Standalones related to the Hawks MC
Out of the Blue (Lan, Easton, and Parker's story)
Out Gamed (novella) (Nancy and Gamer's story)
Outplayed (novella) (Violet and Travis's story)
Out to Find Freedom (Emerson and Warden's story)

.

Romantic comedies

Making Changes

Making Sense

Fumbled Love

Trinity Love Series

Left to Chance

Love of Liberty (novella)

Paranormal

Death (with Justine Littleton)

In The Dark

CONNECT WITH LILA ROSE

Webpage: www.lilarosebooks.com

Facebook: http://bit.ly/2du0taO

Instagram: www.instagram.com/lilarose78/

Goodreads:
www.goodreads.com/author/show/7236200.Lila_Rose